Running Scared

Thomas J. Dygard

William Morrow & Company/New York/1977

Printed in the United States of America.
Design by Victoria Gomez.
1 2 3 4 5 6 7 8 9 10

Library of Congress Cataloging in Publication Data

Dygard, Thomas J
Running scared.
SUMMARY: A football coach whose job is on the line discovers a talented quarterback who is afraid to run.
[1. Football—Fiction] I. Title.
PZ7.D9893Ru [Fic] 76-56862
ISBN 0-688-22103-3
ISBN 0-688-32103-8 lib. bdg.

Running Scared

chapter 1

Coach Chuck Pearce walked across the Marlin State campus, heading toward the field house where his football players would be changing into their practice uniforms in another hour for the afternoon's drill.

The bright September sunshine was warm, but the air had the snap of autumn in it. The campus was coming alive for the new school year, with students milling around the registration offices, visiting their classrooms, and lining up in the bookstore.

From his own days as a student at Marlin State, Pearce knew the feelings of the young men and women signing up for their courses, meeting their instructors, looking over their dormitory rooms. In September, the slate was clean.

As a football coach, Pearce experienced the same feeling—a sense of a new beginning, with high hopes—each September.

"In September, every team is a championship team," was one of the sayings of the football coaching profession.

Pearce frowned at the thought of the word *championship*. He was hearing it too often these days from the members of the alumni association.

Just this morning, the executive committee of the alumni association had bandied the word around—*championship*—as if all the games already had been won. The occasion was the annual preseason meeting to plan the weekly football luncheons and work out ticket distribution problems.

"This is our year, Chuck," one of the members had said, beaming. "I can feel it in my bones."

Pearce had frowned.

The report of the ticket committee's chairman—"more season-ticket requests than ever before in Marlin State's history"—brought a round of applause and knowing smiles from everyone at the table.

"How about that, Chuck?" the chairman of the ticket committee asked.

"I hope they're not disappointed," Pearce said.

Some of the members of the executive committee looked at Pearce quizzically, obviously puzzled by his reluctance to join wholeheartedly in their gleeful anticipation of a triumphant season.

Henry Osgood, the president of the alumni association, broke the moment of silence. "All football coaches are pessimists," he said. "They're born that way."

Pearce had glanced at Osgood and had seen the alumni president eyeing him closely through his wire-rimmed glasses.

Turning the corner at the library and heading toward the last block to the field house, Pearce was only mildly surprised when he saw Henry Osgood's car parked at the curb.

"Well, here we go," he said aloud.

It wasn't that Henry Osgood's automobile was an unusual sight around the field house. As president of the Marlin State Alumni Association, Osgood regularly attended the practice sessions. But today he was more than an hour early for practice. Coming in the wake of the alumni association's executive-committee meeting this morning, and with the season's first game less than three weeks away, Pearce did not find it difficult to imagine why Henry Osgood was appearing at the field house at this hour.

Pearce covered the remaining block to the field house and skipped up the four concrete steps to the front door. He walked in and turned down the steps to the basement where his small office was located.

Henry Osgood was standing in a corridor in the basement, looking at the bulletin board. Along with the practice schedules and other notices, the bulletin board was dotted with letters from former players and old grads living out of town, wishing the team well in the coming season.

"Hello, Henry."

"Hello, Chuck. Got a minute before practice?"

"Sure. C'mon in."

Pearce led the way into the small room that served as his office and closed the door. He circled around behind the desk and sat down in a straight-back wooden chair, tilting the chair until it leaned comfortably against the wall.

Osgood sat in the office's only other chair. "Chuck, this is a bit awkward."

"Yes . . .?"

"Chuck, you know that I was the one who pulled your name out of the hat six years ago when Marlin State needed a new football coach."

Yes, Chuck Pearce knew. Henry Osgood had been chairman of the selection committee charged with finding a coach to lead Marlin State out of the dark days of defeat and back to the football glory days. The Tigers had not fielded a winner in ten years, not since Chuck Pearce himself played on the team as an all-conference tackle. Pearce had moved from Marlin State to the professional football ranks and seemed on the edge of stardom when an injury washed him out as a player forever. Henry Osgood's search for a coach and Chuck Pearce's search for a new career crossed paths. It was a miracle of timing. The man and the job seemed made for each other, the perfect match. A Marlin State alumnus would lead the Tigers back to the top. For Pearce, the chance to return to his home state and his alma mater in Indiana as football coach was a new lease on life, coming as it did when he was in the depths of depression over the end of his playing career. The alumni had greeted Pearce like a conquering hero, back in his homeland to rebuild the team. They handed him an open-ended contract and all their support.

"We never minced words," Osgood continued.

"The deal from the start, you know, was that we would give you all of our support and you would produce a winner."

Pearce nodded.

Yes, Marlin State had hired Chuck Pearce to produce a winner. Pearce had done that, in one sense. He had never had a losing season. But he had never delivered a championship either. And he knew that what the alumni association had meant by a winner was not just a winning record but the championship of the State Intercollegiate Athletic Association. And six years was a long time. Perhaps long enough.

"Chuck, putting it on the line, we feel that we have given you the lineup to win the championship this year."

Osgood and the other alumni were not far from right. Pearce knew that his Marlin State team was shaping up to be the best in his six years at the helm. From end to end, the line was solid rock on defense and dynamite on offense. In the backfield the Tigers had Winnie the Pooh at one halfback. Winnie's mother had named him Winston Joseph Hardman, but the fact had been long forgotten among teammates and fans. And the Tigers had Burlington T. Johnson at the other halfback. Both were good, fast flankers and good pass receivers. And at fullback the

Tigers had Louie Stetson, as strong as they come at 215 pounds and fast enough to get the job done on anybody's team.

It was easy to see why Henry Osgood and the other alumni were excited about the prospects. They saw the makings of a championship team, maybe undefeated, perhaps going to one of the small-college postseason bowl games. And after all those dark years of losing and then the years of coming close with Chuck Pearce, their hunger for a championship only served to heighten their hopes.

But Chuck Pearce was facing a fact that the alumni could afford to overlook in their preseason jubilation. The Marlin State Tigers had only Harry Willis at quarterback, and that meant nobody to throw the long bomb for a touchdown or complete the short bullet pass when the occasion called for it, and nobody to deliver the brilliant fake that would enable Louie Stetson to make that extra yard against an off-balance lineman. And, as important as all the rest, it meant that there was nobody on the field to give the team the extra something that makes the impossible come true. That is what every great football team has got to have—the one extra yard, the one miracle pass completion at the critical moment, the big play that turns defeat into victory.

And Harry Willis would not be able to do it. A dedicated and hardworking player, a senior hoping to end his Marlin State career in a blaze of glory, Harry Willis lacked the spark of greatness that the Tigers desperately needed at quarterback—and the coach knew it. So did everybody else, even if the alumni preferred to ignore the problem at present. They seemed to view it as a minor problem for Chuck Pearce to solve—nothing more.

"You know that I have no complaints about the support of the alumni," Pearce said. "Their recruiting work has been little short of fantastic."

Pearce meant what he said. It had been the work of the alumni that kept Louie Stetson in town to play for Marlin State instead of going to Notre Dame or Michigan. The alumni had appealed to Louie's local pride, and they had used the good argument that Louie would be coming back to Marlin to earn his living after graduation, and this was where he owed his allegiance. And Bruno Chinigo, the best linebacker in the whole Midwest, lined up with Marlin State because the alumni convinced him that Chuck Pearce was the perfect teacher to train him for professional football. All down the roster, similar stories were behind the names of the players wearing the Marlin State uniform.

"But, Henry, you know and I know that we've got a serious weakness at quarterback," Pearce said. "It could be a fatal weakness."

Osgood started to speak, but Pearce waved him off. "I'm not trying to make excuses in advance for not going all the way to the championship this year," Pearce said. "And I'm not blaming the alumni because they haven't brought me a Bart Starr or a Joe Namath. But it simply is a fact that we don't have a championship quarterback. And mighty few teams win a championship without a topflight quarterback."

Osgood leaned forward. "Harry Willis is a senior. He's experienced . . . ."

"He's not a good passer, not a good ball handler, and he never will be," Pearce said. "I would not say that in public for a million bucks. But it's the truth. Incidentally, Harry knows it."

"I must say that I can't understand your accepting the fact of his shortcomings that way—and allowing Harry Willis himself to accept them," Osgood said curtly.

Pearce looked at Osgood without saying anything.

"You've had him for four years," Osgood said. "In four years, with good coaching, a player is supposed to develop."

Pearce felt a brief flare of anger. Then he smiled,

trying to put on a friendly face. "Henry," he said slowly, "I'm not making excuses. Yes, perhaps another coach could have made Harry Willis into a great quarterback. I doubt it, but it's possible. I'm just telling you this so you will understand exactly how things stack up."

Osgood straightened himself a bit in the chair. "Chuck, the alumni have supported you. They have waited, and pretty patiently, I might add, for six years. They feel that this is the year to fish or cut bait. Some of the fellows thought that I should talk to you about it. After all, I was the one who first picked you for the job, and now I'm the president of the alumni association." He paused. "You know that I wish you all the luck in the world."

"I understand what you're saying," Pearce said, standing up. "But now if I don't get out there on the practice field, luck won't count for anything at all."

chapter 2

When Chuck Pearce walked onto the practice field, his assistant, Cody Benson, already had the squad working on calisthenics at the south end.

Forty men, Pearce thought, when he looked at the team lined up at the end of the field. Somewhere in the State Intercollegiate Athletic Association this year a team is going to win a championship. Right now, on all nine campuses, the teams were probably doing the same thing, taking their warm-up calisthenics. But at least one of those teams had a special man—one man—who was the quarterback, and he would make the difference through the long season. They would win a game because they had him, and another team would lose a game because they didn't have him, and that would make the difference in the final season's standings and would win the SIAA championship. Such a small part of the whole, just one man. But he would make all the difference in the world. And Chuck Pearce would be a success or a failure because of it. And, Pearce thought, Louie Stetson or Bruno Chinigo would have a good chance at making Little All-America, or would fail to make it, largely because of the team's record. That's just the way things worked. And the team's record would depend on the man playing quarterback for this team. And, Pearce thought, that good quarterback isn't here with us.

The squad had broken up now, and Cody was dividing them into units. One group was working on kicks and kick returns. Another unit was running offense plays. And another blocking one-on-one in a defensive drill.

Pearce thought about the first game, less than three weeks away, with Central Teachers. If Central

Teachers had a strong team, it would be the first time. They'd get by Teachers without trouble, with Louie Stetson rushing for more than a hundred yards and scoring two touchdowns. Nobody needed an outstanding quarterback to do a job on Teachers.

Pearce looked from one unit to another, the unit working on kicking and kick returns, the unit working on offensive plays, and the unit working on defense, and he thought, Forty players, and it's got to be trimmed to thirty-five players, to meet the strict requirements of the SIAA. "Thirty-five players is ridiculous," he said to himself. "Nobody can have a football squad of thirty-five players." But then he had to draw himself up short. That very restriction was what made the SIAA such a select group among football coaches. All over the country, in the collegiate ranks and among the professionals, they knew that if you could make a consistent winner out of a squad of thirty-five players—none of them receiving much in the way of grants—you could really coach and you could really judge your talent. That was part of what had drawn Chuck Pearce back to Marlin State six year ago, and now it was part of what made him want to stay.

Thursday, and this was already Tuesday, came the deadline for giving the conference the names of the thirty-five players who would make up the Marlin State squad this year. He had to make his cut by tomorrow, at the latest.

Pearce's reverie was interrupted by a football hitting the ground at his feet and bouncing beyond him onto the cinder track. He turned his gaze and watched the ball bound crazily and started to step after it.

"I'll get it."

Pearce looked up and saw a young man in a slipover sweater bend and pick up the ball. The young man looked at the ball in his hands for a moment and then cocked his right arm and fired it across to Harry Willis.

Pearce stared at him. "Would you mind doing that again?"

The young man laughed.

"Hey, Harry," Pearce shouted. "Send that ball back over here a minute."

Harry Willis lofted the ball—a typical Willis pass, floating high, one of the type that's marked "sure interception." Pearce caught it and handed the ball to the young man in the slipover sweater.

"Here," he said. "Throw it to that guy over there again."

The young man laughed again, looked at the ball

in his right hand, cocked, and threw quickly on a straight line to Willis.

"What's your name?"

"Larry Hudson."

"I don't need to ask if you've ever played football before."

"I used to play a little," he said. "In high school. But I gave up after that."

"You must be a freshman."

"No, I'm a sophomore."

"I don't think I've seen you before," Pearce said. "Marlin State is small enough so that not many faces go unnoticed around here in the course of a year."

Larry had the clean-cut look of everybody's all-American boy—a strong chin, a bit of heavy brow over steady blue eyes, and close-cropped blond hair. Pearce thought it was the kind of fresh, handsome face that a person doesn't fail to notice and doesn't forget.

"I'm new this year," Larry said with a smile. "I transferred in from Southern Cal."

"You're a long way from home."

"My family lives in Minnesota, so I'm really a Midwesterner," Larry said. "There was a sort of tradition that we went to Southern Cal." He paused. "I guess you could say that I'm breaking the family tradition."

Pearce forced his attention away from the distracting thoughts that had come to him and said, "Oh, I see. Well, let me say welcome to Marlin State."

"Thanks, Coach, and good luck," Larry said. He walked on past the practice field and turned behind a building.

Pearce watched him walk away. The young man had the stride of a natural athlete, the effortless, almost casual movement and the sort of gentle spring in his step that made you think he might leap suddenly at any moment. He had the physique of a running back—broad, thick shoulders, small waist, narrow hips.

"Hey, Bruno, quit loafing out there," Pearce shouted, as he walked onto the practice field and took charge of the drills.

That night it was after eight o'clock before Pearce got home. He had kept the players on the field until six o'clock, and then he and Cody had gone over the squad list making their first tentative cuts to the conference limit of thirty-five players. They would have to make their final decisions first thing in the morning.

Maggie had kept his dinner in the oven, and she took it out and put it on the table when she saw the car pull into the driveway.

"How'd it go today?"

"Okay. Nobody broke a leg."

Pearce sat down to eat his dinner, and Maggie got herself a cup of coffee and sat down with him at the table in the dining alcove.

"You're not the most talkative guy in the world," she said finally.

"Sorry. I was thinking of something else."

"I think you're going to tell me that somebody did break a leg, after all."

Pearce laughed. "No, but we were working on the cuts tonight. That's always tough."

He lapsed into silence again, then got up abruptly and said, "Excuse me a moment. I've got to make a telephone call."

"But you haven't finished. It'll get cold. What's wrong?"

"Nothing's wrong, believe me, honey. Just something I can't get out of my head. I'll be right back."

Pearce walked into the den, closed the door, and sat down at his desk. He stared at the telephone for a moment, then lifted the receiver.

Ten minutes later he had located the dormitory where a transfer student named Larry Hudson was living, and he had a student hailing Hudson to the phone.

"Larry?"

"Yes, this is Larry Hudson."

"Larry, this is Coach Pearce. I'd like to talk to you in my office in the morning. Could you come by?"

"I guess so. I've got a break at ten o'clock. Would that be all right? Is there . . .?"

"That'll be fine, ten o'clock. I'll see you then."

"Can you tell me . . .?"

"Let's talk in the morning, Larry. I appreciate your giving me the time. See you then. Okay?"

"Okay."

chapter 3

At ten o'clock the next morning Chuck Pearce was seated in the straight-back chair, tilted back against the wall, behind his desk in his office.

"Coach?" Larry Hudson poked his head in the door.

"C'mon in, Larry. Close the door, will you? Have a seat."

Larry had a couple of books in his hand, and he settled them on his lap when he sat down in the other straight-back chair across the desk from Pearce. He looked expectantly at the coach.

"Larry, I'll come right to the point. I'd like you to come out for the team."

Pearce could see that Larry wasn't surprised. He was sure Larry had seen the request coming a mile away after the telephone call last night. Pearce tried to read the reaction in Larry's eyes, but Larry hardly blinked and didn't reveal his feelings in any way. Pearce hoped that his own feelings weren't showing. For one thing, he felt out of place asking Larry Hudson to come out for the team—or asking anyone to come out for the team. It was an unwritten rule that the player, and not the coach, asked for the opportunity. Oh, sure there was recruiting, in which the coach made it clear that the school and the team wanted the boy. But that was different from approaching a student who already had chosen the school and asking him to join the team. Pearce was coming close to promising a spot on the team, something that wasn't done even in the heat of recruiting. The request to Larry could lead to a troublesome coach-player relationship, and Pearce knew it. He guessed that Larry Hudson knew it too. Pearce also knew he was courting a serious morale problem by inviting a late arrival to beat Harry Willis out of the quarterback job in Harry's senior year. And he was risking all of this because of a conclusion that he had drawn from seeing two passes thrown across the practice field. Sure, Pearce told himself, it would be taking a big chance in a lot of different ways. But he had decided it was a chance worth taking. At this time yesterday, Pearce had reconciled himself to being a coach with a great team, but no quarterback. And now, today, he had a hope, if only a slim hope, of being a coach with a great team, period.

"Coach," Larry said, appearing to choose his words carefully, "I played football in high school, but I've never thought of . . . I mean, I haven't played in college, and I haven't planned to . . . ."

"You could."

Larry paused. "It's a personal thing, Coach. Besides, you only saw me throw a couple of passes."

"My players leave it up to me to measure their capabilities," Pearce said. "It's my profession."

"I didn't mean . . . well, Coach, yes, I guess I could play. I mean I could if I wanted to. But I don't want to play." Larry looked straight into Pearce's eyes. "And you don't want a quarterback who doesn't want to play."

Pearce returned his gaze. "No, you're right. I wouldn't want a quarterback who didn't want to play."

They looked at each other for a moment without speaking.

Larry broke the brief silence. "Okay, Coach, I'll lay the cards on the table."

"I'd appreciate it," Pearce said.

"I'm afraid I'll get hurt," Larry said. "It doesn't sound good to say it, but that's the fact of the matter. I'm afraid. That's all there is to it. There's nothing I can do about it."

Pearce stared at him a moment. "You're mighty strong looking to be worrying about getting hurt."

"I told you that it doesn't sound good to say it. I didn't want to say it." He took a deep breath. "I just never should have picked up that ball at the practice field yesterday." He smiled weakly.

"It doesn't jibe, Larry."

"What doesn't jibe?"

"I don't know you well at all, and I won't pretend that I do, but I'd be willing to bet that you love the game of football."

Larry started to speak, but Pearce waved him off. "You were hanging around the practice field. Nobody does that who hates the game and is frightened by it. And when you zinged that pass to Harry Willis . . . well, you darned near fondled the ball, and you smiled when you threw it. You loved it. That's what doesn't jibe."

Larry shrugged. "Jibe or not, it's true," he said. "It's not easy for me to face. But the fact is that I'm afraid I'll be hurt."

Pearce looked at Larry, saying nothing, waiting for Larry to continue, hoping that Larry would continue. Behind the simply stated fact that he was afraid to play football there had to be a reason.

Finally, Larry broke the silence. "It's not the sort of thing that I go around talking about," he said.

Pearce waited.

"It's very personal," Larry said. "And I hope that I can count on you to keep our conversation private."

Pearce decided not to press further. Larry clearly was not ready to discuss his fears or the reasons for them. Pearce could imagine the ordeal involved for Larry in the single step of admitting his fears to a stranger—and a football coach, at that. No, this was not the time to probe further.

"Don't worry," Pearce said. He smiled, hoping to put Larry at ease. "Don't worry. It's private."

Pearce stood and extended his hand, and Larry took it. Their eyes met as they shook hands.

"Just a couple of other points for you to keep in mind," Pearce said. "One, everybody's got something he's afraid of. You, me, everybody—we've all got something we fear. The mark of a man is trying to defeat those fears instead of knuckling under."

"I know," Larry said softly.

"And," Pearce said, as he walked around the desk and opened the office door for Larry, "if you think you might change your mind, you'll have to be quick about it, because my eligibility list is due at the conference office tomorrow."

Larry let the remark slide off and said, "Thanks, Coach, and good luck."

"Good luck to you too, Larry."

Pearce walked out the door and into the corridor with Larry and watched him go up the steps to the main floor.

Back inside his office, Pearce sat down at his desk. He picked up a pencil and doodled on a piece of paper. He could not shake from his mind the two vivid pictures of Larry Hudson—one, the beautiful fluid movement as he passed the football; and two, the face with the downcast eyes as he explained he could not play because he was afraid.

Pearce knew that Larry's secret could be broken easily enough. It would be no problem to find out from the registrar's office where Larry had graduated from high school. And then one telephone call to the high-school coach would unravel the mystery. Pearce was tempted. He glanced at the telephone on his desk. But he did not pick it up. No, he decided, Larry had to choose the time for the coach to know the reasons—if ever. For now, at least, Larry would have to call the shots.

Pearce drew aimless swirls on the pad for another ten minutes, and then dialed his assistant's office.

"Cody, cut one more name off that eligibility list," he said. "I've got a new one to add."

"Oh, who?"

"Larry Hudson."

"Larry who?"

"I'll tell you about it at lunch. Right now I've got to tell Larry Hudson about it."

chapter 4

"Larry, I've got an idea, and I want to make you a proposition," Chuck Pearce said.

"Sure, Coach," Larry said. He smiled.

The two were standing beneath a large elm tree in front of the Science Building, barely an hour after their first meeting in Pearce's office. Students were streaming out of the building and walking past them, heading for their noon break in the day's classes. Several nodded to the coach, a well-known figure on the Marlin State campus, but none of the students walking by were hailing Larry. He had been walking alone when he emerged from the building, too. Larry was a new face on the campus, a transfer student who had not yet slipped into the easy classroom friendships the other sophomores carried over from last year.

Pearce looked at Larry intently and paused a moment. He hoped that his face was not revealing the anxiety he felt. He had sounded certain, he knew, when he told Cody Benson to make room for another name on the list. Pearce's idea had seemed great when it first ran through his mind. Larry could not refuse. He would have to accept. But now Pearce knew that Larry could, of course, say no.

"Come out for the team as a passer," Pearce said.

"Coach, I . . . ."

"You didn't hear me right, Larry. I said, as a passer. You won't have to scrimmage. You won't have to run the ball in a game. You'll just throw. That's all, just pass."

"What?"

"Just throw," Pearce repeated. "Be a passing specialist. Nothing new about the idea, really. Teams have had kicking specialists for years. And in the pros, they protect their passers from physical contact as much as possible. It's smart. No team with a good passer wants to lose him to an injury in some unnecessary physical contact." Pearce paused. "And now Marlin State is going to have a passing specialist."

"What would the team think of a quarterback who's afraid to run the ball?"

"I'll handle that. I'm the coach."

Pearce thought he detected a glint of interest in Larry's eyes.

"But, Coach, I haven't played . . . ."

"Passing a football is just like swimming and bicycle riding," Pearce said with a smile. "If you ever master the art, you never lose it."

Larry laughed. "Do you really think . . .?"

"I'm sure of it. What do you say?"

"Okay."

That afternoon, when the stranger named Larry Hudson showed up for practice without fanfare or explanation, Pearce could sense the questions in the minds of his players.

Not that a new face in the preseason drills was anything out of the ordinary at Marlin State. Students who caught the football fever occasionally decided on the spur of the moment to try out for the team. They seldom lasted long. Most of them dropped out after a couple of grinding practice sessions under the hot September sun. The others, with rare exception, vanished when Pearce had to cut the squad to the conference limit.

But this newcomer was joining the team in the third week of practice. It was a time when most of the walk-ons had come and gone. Also, it was the very day the coach was making his final decisions on cutting the squad. Every year the players watched the deadline carefully. To a man, they were worried about the cutback, either for their own future with the team or that of a friend with marginal talent. And Pearce knew that the obvious point was not lost on his players: somebody was being trimmed from the squad to make room for the untried transfer student.

Pearce said nothing, letting the players' unasked questions go unanswered. It was important to postpone the reaction to a quarterback who wouldn't run the ball until the team could see his value as a passer.

Beyond the players, Pearce's main concern centered on the questions that Bill Oliver, the savvy little sports editor of the *Marlin Herald*, would be asking. For the moment not only Larry Hudson's secret fears but also his tremendous passing abilities needed to be kept under wraps. So far Marlin State was being billed as a great team without a great quarterback, a fatal flaw. Scouting in the State Intercollegiate Athletic Association was confined to the big games. Nobody scouted anybody's practice sessions. So Pearce was safe with his secret weapon, unless Bill Oliver made a headline out of Larry Hudson. The other coaches did read the papers.

Squinting through his wire-rim glasses riding low on his nose, Oliver didn't miss much in his daily visits to the Marlin State practice field. And, sure enough, it didn't take Oliver long to focus his attention on the stranger engaged in the unusual practice activity behind the goalposts.

Larry, wearing a sweatsuit instead of pads and a practice uniform, was taking the snap from Harold Temple, a third-string center, fading back, and passing to Byron Farr, a third-string end. No question, Larry was acting like a quarterback—and a pretty special one at that, engaging in his own private drill session apart from the rest of the team.

"Who's that?" Oliver asked, suddenly appearing beside Pearce.

Pearce was tempted to lay the cards on the table for Oliver. The sports editor always had been a friend of his and a supporter of the Marlin State team. He could be trusted with the secret of the stranger in the sweatsuit down behind the goalposts. But through Pearce's six years as head coach of the Marlin State Tigers, he had never confided in Oliver, and Oliver never had pressed Pearce to reveal plans or break a confidence. Oliver seemed to understand that certain information about the Tigers should not be published. He never had broken the unspoken agreement. It had been a good relationship. And now Pearce decided he would bet on Oliver's continuing the good relationship.

"Who's who?" Pearce asked innocently.

"The kid who is throwing to Byron."

"Oh, that one. His name is Larry Hudson."

"Where'd he come from?"

"He's a transfer student," Pearce said, trying to sound matter-of-fact. "From some school out West."

"With that kind of passing, I'd guess he must have transferred in from the Los Angeles Rams."

Pearce laughed and walked away, but Oliver followed him.

"What's going on here, Chuck? Have you got a quarterback you've been hiding?"

"I don't know, Bill, and that's the honest truth."

This time Pearce succeeded in walking away from the sports editor.

chapter 5

It was a strange couple of weeks, starting with the day that Larry first showed up. Everybody noticed, of course, when the new man didn't dress out in pads and a practice uniform. Instead he pulled on a sweat-suit, ran through the calisthenics with the team, and then adjourned to the end of the field to take the snap from Harold Temple and fade back for a pass to Byron Farr.

"So he's getting in shape," said Louie Stetson.

At the end of the first day of the passing session behind the goalposts, Byron held forth in a corner of the dressing room, speaking with his usual exuberance.

"Wow!" he said. "Let me tell you, that guy knows how to throw! He could make an all-American flanker out of me. He's on the button every time, let me tell you. And with zip, real zip."

For four days, Larry spent the practice sessions behind the goalposts, taking the snap from center and fading back and throwing to Byron—with deadly accuracy and bullet speed. Again everybody noticed, including Harry Willis, who was directing the first-string offense unit in practice, but nobody said anything.

Then Pearce hailed Larry onto the practice field for a series of plays with the first-string offense unit near the end of the day's drills. Carefully Pearce had waited until Bill Oliver had departed to write his day's story. No point in stretching Oliver's cooperative attitude to the breaking point.

Larry moved into the slot easily, calling the basic hand-off plays and throwing one short pass, moving the team down the field without a hitch.

Pearce watched his squad and wondered what was going through their minds.

"You'd better tell them what's up," Cody said.

"Not quite yet," Pearce replied.

But the next day after practice, Pearce called Bruno Chinigo, the linebacker who was the team captain, into his office. "Larry Hudson has got everyone wondering, hasn't he, Bruno?"

"Yes, sir."

Pearce smiled. "And Larry's not talking much either, is he?"

"No, sir."

"He's playing it the way I asked him to," Pearce said.

"Yes, sir."

"Tell me what the players are wondering, Bruno."

"He looks like a whale of a passer, and Winnie says he's smoother on the hand-offs than any quarterback he ever saw."

"That's not what I mean, Bruno," Pearce said, looking at Bruno sharply

"Yes, sir," Bruno said. He took a deep breath. "They're wondering about having somebody new who is, well, you know, special. He showed up late. You know, wasn't here when practice started. Just showed up one day, you know. And he doesn't wear pads and he doesn't scrimmage. It's, well, like he was too special to take a chance on getting hurt. And I guess he's made the cut by this time, hasn't he? Harry Willis is wondering, too, you know."

"Yes, Bruno, I know," Pearce said softly. He paused and leaned back in his chair until it tilted against the wall. "Bruno, how much does Mitch Reynolds practice?"

Mitch Reynolds was Marlin State's place kicker, a frail little guy with a deadly aim and tremendous dedication. He had made himself into a college varsity football player by going out for the only position he could hope for—kicking specialist.

"Well," Bruno said, puzzled by the sudden shift in the conversation, "Mitch takes his warm-ups and then he works on his kicking."

"He doesn't wear pads, does he?"

"No."

"He doesn't scrimmage, does he?"

"No."

"Well?"

"Coach, it's different with a quarterback. Just different."

"Bruno, it's no different at all in this particular case. We have ourselves a passing specialist. A superb passer, I might add. You said so yourself—he's a whale of a passer. I am not going to take any chances with his physical health any more than I would with

Mitch's health. It's my decision, and that is the way we're going to do it."

"Okay, Coach."

"There's more to it than that, Bruno, and this is very important. Larry Hudson is one of us on this team, and he's playing it my way. You know how important that is. Everybody in the world knows that we need a passer to go all the way to the championship this year. I want you to explain it to the team. You're the captain. They'll listen to you. I'm making you responsible for seeing to it that my decision in this matter is supported by the team."

"Yes, sir."

In the days leading up to the opening game against Central Teachers, Pearce saw evidence that Bruno had done his job well, as Pearce had known he would, explaining to the players what Larry Hudson could mean to the team. The only hint of discontent came from Winnie the Pooh, the flanker back who ran and leaped like a deer and could catch anybody's pass if it came within ten yards of him.

"What's with you?" Bruno fired back at him, when he heard Winnie complaining. "Do you want to scrimmage at linebacker to prove you can play flanker back? Hell, no, you don't. You want to work at your own position. But you're saying that Larry

Hudson ought to run the ball in practice to prove he's a passer. Isn't that right?"

Before Winnie could come back with a rejoinder, Louie Stetson spoke up. "Look, Winnie, I don't want to have to practice at linebacker, and you don't cither." Everyone laughed.

The problem was settled, at least for the time being. But Pearce knew, when he heard about the episode, that there might be rough sledding ahead.

Before the game with Central Teachers, Pearce talked to Larry. "We're not going to need you today, and I don't intend to play you," he said. "We'll save your unveiling for another day."

Larry nodded.

Nobody on the team said anything when Pearce announced the starting lineup with Harry Willis at quarterback, but Pearce noticed some glances among the players.

Central Teachers turned out to be not the slightest bit tougher than expected. But after the game, as Pearce walked toward the dressing room with the 42-7 final count glowing on the scoreboard at the north end of the field, his brow was furrowed with a frown. The game had showed him, more than ever, how much his Tigers needed the passing and ball-handling expertise of Larry Hudson.

True, the Marlin State Tigers had dealt the Central Teachers a severe thrashing, and they had done so without Larry Hudson ever getting into the game. He remained a mystery—to the team, to the press, and, most important of all, to the other teams in the conference.

Bill Oliver had mentioned Larry in his stories on the practice sessions leading up to the Central Teachers game. But he always identified Larry as a transfer student who had joined the team as a quarterback late in the preseason drills. He also added that Harry Willis was continuing to direct the first-team offense in scrimmage. So now, with the first game over, Larry Hudson's name still had escaped notice. The player wearing number eleven on his jersey still had not been seen. Pearce, as he walked along head down, measured the good against the bad. There had been plenty of good things, as witness the lopsided score and the smiles and laughter of the Marlin State players and fans. But there had been bad signs, too.

It had taken only five minutes from the opening kickoff for the Tigers to reach the end zone for their first touchdown. In a way, the march was an awesome display of power, with the Marlin State line knocking back the Central Teachers defenders on every play, Louie Stetson thundering through for large gains, and Winnie the Pooh skittering around the ends behind strong blocking.

But Harry Willis almost gave Pearce a coronary with a wobbly pass at midfield into a nest of Central Teachers defenders. Winnie came racing out of nowhere, leaped higher than anyone else, and speared the ball for a first down on the Central Teachers' thirty-six-yard line. Pearce exhaled in relief and wondered to himself how many of Harry Willis's weak passes the Tigers could survive against a tougher opponent.

Pearce had caught himself glancing at Larry, standing at the sideline, as the Tigers rolled downfield. Larry's genuine admiration was obvious when Winnie the Pooh made a first-down catch out of what, by all odds, should have been an interception. Winnie the Pooh had leaped into the air for the ball and whipped them all.

When the offensive unit came off the field after the touchdown, Larry joined the crowd of sideliners patting them on the back. He pounded an excited Harry Willis on the shoulder pads and shouted, "That's the way."

Pearce smiled when he saw the expression on Larry Hudson's face, saying better than words that this was his team and that he wanted to be playing.

Marlin State's tough defense, with Bruno Chinigo dominating the field from his linebacker position, stopped Central Teachers cold. The Teachers had to punt, and Marlin State began moving toward another touchdown from midfield.

This time the scoring drive belonged to Louie Stetson. The powerful fullback steamed up the middle and slashed off the tackles, following his blocking perfectly and crashing over tacklers when the blocking ran out. It was fitting that Louie was the one who got the call on the one-yard line, and he hit the middle and scored the touchdown.

Larry met Louie at the sideline, shook his hand, and mumbled something, and Louie nodded in acknowledgment and smiled.

Pearce noticed the gesture. He was pleased to see Larry viewing Winnie the Pooh and Louie Stetson with the high regard they so richly deserved. Winnie the Pooh and Louie were important cogs in the Marlin State football machine, and it was important that Larry be able to work with them smoothly, if he was going to be the quarterback.

But despite the touchdown, Pearce had seen the flaws in the attack being directed by Harry Willis. In the heat of the touchdown drive, the fans didn't notice. Perhaps most of the players didn't notice. But

Pearce saw Harry stumble slightly on a hand-off, knocking off the timing, and Louie Stetson was stopped at the line because of the error. Pearce shuddered, as always, when Harry threw his one pass of the drive. Marlin State was lucky that the ball fell incomplete. Again, the floating ball, completely lacking in zip, was a prime candidate for an interception.

Pearce shook off the bad memories of Harry Willis's performance—the only dark spots in a day of magnificent triumph—and broke into a smile as he turned into the dressing room. The players were still shouting and laughing, and Cody was stretching a banner across the wall: *Now for Warren Tech.*

That game, Pearce knew, would be a sterner test, perhaps the toughest of the season. Warren Tech was a strong and experienced team. Some called the Eagles the preseason favorites to win the SIAA championship.

As one sports editor had put it, "Nobody can stop Warren Tech unless Marlin State comes up with a miracle find to solve the quarterback problem." Pearce had the clipping on his desk.

He was smiling as he waded into the victory celebration with his players.

chapter 6

The bus ride from Marlin State to Warren Tech took only a little over an hour on a bright Saturday morning, and the players trooped into the dressing room at a few minutes after noon.

The air fairly crackled with the tension. Unlike the easy banter that had prevailed before the Central Teachers game a week ago, a grim sort of silence hung over the room as the players pulled on their pads and jerseys. The difference was that today's opponent was Warren Tech, and the Tigers were dressing for the game that the whole conference was watching.

Pearce held a piece of paper in his hand listing the starting lineup. Only he and Cody had seen the list.

When Bill Oliver had approached him after the Thursday practice with his usual request for the starting lineup to use in his story for Friday's paper, Pearce had stalled him off. "You saw the lineup we started last week, didn't you?"

"Are you going with the same starters against Warren Tech?"

"Would you change a lineup that won its first game by a 42-7 score?"

"You're ducking my question."

"That's right, Bill, I am," Pearce said, and that ended the conversation.

At the Friday night pep rally, where the Marlin State tradition dictated that the starting eleven be presented, Pearce had introduced the entire squad, all thirty-five men, without the slightest indication who would be on the starting lineup.

Now Pearce broke the strained silence in the dressing room, clapping his hands and shouting, "Okay, okay, come to life and hear me."

He held the piece of paper in front of him,

although he didn't need it to recite the starting lineup. "At the ends," he began, and read the names, going through the tackles, the guards, the center, the fullback, the halfbacks. "And at quarterback, Larry Hudson."

Pearce let the silence rest for only a moment. "Now let's get out there and rack 'em up, right now, right now, let's go."

The team jogged down the corridor to the field, and Pearce sent a manager to the press box with the starting lineup, the first public indication that Larry Hudson, the player nobody had heard of, would be the man at signal caller.

The move came as no real surprise to the Marlin State players. Every night of the previous week, including a session after the pep rally on Friday night, Pearce and Cody and Larry Hudson and Harry Willis had huddled over the playbook around the dining-room table at Pearce's house. Pearce had brought Willis into the group to give Larry the benefit of the other quarterback's experience with the Marlin State team and his knowledge of the Warren Tech team from the last year's game. Pearce had another motive, too, which was to keep Harry Willis from sinking into complete despondency. This way, Pearce figured, Harry was part of the conspiracy to surprise Warren Tech with a new ingredient in the offense—a passing specialist. And if it worked, Harry would come in for a share of the credit, having made a big contribution to Larry's success. On the practice field during the week, Pearce had worked Larry into backfield drills, having him hand off to Winnie and Burlington T. Johnson and Louie Stetson.

Still, Pearce couldn't be sure how well the team was accepting Larry Hudson, the player who was late coming out for the team, the player who didn't wear pads and didn't scrimmage, the player who now was moving ahead of Harry Willis. Sure, they wanted to win, and they knew that a better quarterback would help them do so, but the aura of "something special" about Larry continued to bother them, and Pearce knew it.

Pearce stepped out of the corridor behind the team, blinking a bit in the bright autumn sunlight. The Warren Tech stadium was filled to capacity. The crowd was noisy and happy, the kind that turns out on a day of gorgeous football weather to root home a winner. The Marlin State fans were seated on the forty-yard line across the field, and they stood and cheered when the Tigers took the field.

Marlin State won the coin toss, and Pearce nodded. He knew it was silly, but he always considered winning the toss to be a good omen, dating back to his playing days in high school. The Tigers chose to receive the opening kickoff.

On the sideline, Larry jogged nervously and watched the kicker approach the ball. Twenty-one other athletes sprang into action as the ball arched over the field, heading for the waiting arms of Burlington T. Johnson.

Johnson, to the left of center, gathered in the kickoff on the seven-yard line and swung to his right, crossing Winnie the Pooh and handing off. The play was one of the new wrinkles Pearce had put into the Marlin State offense for the Warren Tech game. Winnie the Pooh, with his speed, was to race up the sideline behind a wall of blockers while the Warren Tech defenders were changing direction from their pursuit of Johnson.

The roar from the Warren Tech fans was a quick clue that everything was going wrong. Winnie lost the handle on the hand-off. The ball spurted out of his hands, back toward the goal, and Winnie was chasing it. Now he was in the end zone, trying to scoop it up on the run, and the ball squirted loose again, bounding out of the end zone and onto the playing field, where a Warren Tech player fell on it on the four-yard line.

It was Warren Tech's ball on the Marlin State four-yard line with the game less than a minute old.

Pearce knelt on one knee and pulled a blade of grass, stuck it in his mouth, and watched as his defense took the field. He made no move as Winnie the Pooh jogged past him toward the bench. Winnie looked as though he would burst into tears at any moment.

"We'll make it, baby, we'll make it," Larry called to him. Winnie looked at Larry but said nothing.

On the field, Warren Tech lined up. In the Marlin State defense, Bruno Chinigo danced at his linebacker position, trying to read the play, trying to be ready to spring in whichever direction the ball carrier seemed to be going.

Warren Tech's big fullback, number thirty-four, crashed into the middle of the line. Bruno hit him and put the finishing touch on his forward motion. The referee placed the ball down on the one-yard line. Second down and one yard to go for a touchdown.

Warren Tech came out of the huddle and ran the same play, with the big fullback charging into the middle. This time he got nothing, with Bruno stopping him at the line.

Pearce waved to Bruno, signaling that the next

Warren Tech charge probably would go to the outside, around the ends.

Pearce was right. The quarterback faked to the big fullback in the middle, turned, and pitched far out to a halfback galloping to the left. The halfback was on the five-yard line when he pulled in the ball and, to everybody's surprise, cut inside instead of going for the corner. He caught the Marlin State defense going against the grain. Bruno caught him at the goal, but one step too late.

With the kick the score read Warren Tech 7, Marlin State 0, and less than three minutes of the game were gone.

Warren Tech's kickoff arched high, in the direction of Winnie—was that on purpose?—and Winnie circled slightly under the ball as he waited for it.

Winnie gathered in the ball and cut to his right to cross with Johnson. This time Winnie held onto the ball instead of handing off to Johnson, and the strategy worked. Warren Tech's defenders slowed ever so slightly, but they slowed nevertheless, to see which man would come out of the crossover with the ball. Winnie raced to the sideline, heading upfield for the shelter of a wall of blockers. The momentary hesitation of the on-rushing defenders, plus the good blocking and Winnie's own speed, popped Winnie loose for a forty-seven-yard return to the Warren Tech forty-four-yard line, where Winnie finally was knocked out of bounds.

Larry peeled off his parka and jogged onto the field to set up the huddle.

Across the field, the appearance of the strange number eleven at quarterback, in place of the expected Harry Willis wearing number fourteen, did not go unnoticed. Warren Tech's coach was having a hurried conference with an assistant. On the field, Warren Tech's defensive signal caller shrugged his shoulders in response to the questioning looks from his teammates.

Pearce, down on one knee on the sideline with a blade of grass in his mouth, watched Larry move into the huddle.

Larry called the play, clapped his hands, and moved the team into position. He stepped up to the center and looked at the defense spreading out before him. Behind him, Louie Stetson and Burlington T. Johnson crouched. And to his right, Winnie the Pooh settled into the flanker position.

Larry took the snap and backpedaled quickly, scanning the field of his receivers. To his right, Winnie faked left, faked right, cut left and zipped across the field, about twelve yards downfield, parallel to the line of scrimmage, waving his right hand high above his head. Larry fired a bullet pass, right on the mark, and Winnie pulled it in without breaking stride and veered downfield.

The play got the Tigers seventeen yards, to the Warren Tech twenty-seven-yard line.

Warren Tech called time out.

On the sideline, Pearce smiled and sent Harry Willis into the game, replacing Larry Hudson.

Willis handed off to Louie Stetson, who ran off tackle for eight yards, and pitched out to Winnie for four and a first down on the Warren Tech fifteen-yard line.

Pearce waved again, and Larry went into the game. Pearce smiled. Everything was working so far. He had that wonderful feeling of being one step ahead of the coach across the field. He was going to try to get two steps ahead in the game of trying to outguess each other.

Larry called the play in the huddle, clapped his hands, and walked into the lineup behind the center.

He took the snap and began backpedaling and—suddenly, surprisingly—slipped the ball to his left in a pitchout to Winnie the Pooh. The Warren Tech secondary was already falling back for the pass. The onrushing linemen, looking for a deep drop back, overshot Larry. Winnie the Pooh turned on the speed and went all the way, tightroping down the sideline to the goal.

Mitch Reynolds's kick made the score 7-7.

Following the ensuing kickoff, Marlin State's defense, with Bruno Chinigo making tackles all over the field, held Warren Tech deep in the Eagles' own territory and forced them to punt.

As Winnie the Pooh and Burlington T. Johnson skipped backward to await the punt, a sort of electricity was evident among the Marlin State players. Those on the field and those on the bench knew that the first quarter was drawing to a close and the highly touted Eagles hadn't mustered a single threatening move on offense. True, they had a touchdown. But it was a fluke, a fumble that handed them the touchdown. They hadn't been able to move the ball the first time they had possession in a real scrimmage situation. And Marlin State, on the other hand, had marched to a touchdown in its first possession. Everybody was ready to do so again and confident that they could.

The snap from center was perfect, and the punter, on his own goal line, got the kick away in beautiful form. The spiral soared into the clear autumn sky. Burlington T. Johnson waved Winnie the Pooh away and circled under the ball on the Marlin State forty-five-yard line. He caught it and was nailed immediately.

Larry Hudson shucked his parka and jogged onto the field.

On the sideline, Chuck Pearce continued to kneel on one knee, chewing a blade of grass, the very picture of composure and calm confidence. But inside everything was churning. This was the big one. Sure, he thought, we caught them off-balance when Larry first appeared and rifled a perfect pass to Winnie. Nobody in the world, including Warren Tech, had had the slightest inkling that Marlin State could unfurl a deadly passing attack. But now the Warren Tech coaches and players knew that Marlin State had the weapon, and there had been time for them to make their adjustments. This was going to be a big series of downs, against a Warren Tech team that wasn't going to let one touchdown settle the decision. Now, from here on out, Pearce thought, we'll find out what we can do when the receivers have a tougher time getting free and when the linemen are having a harder time protecting Larry.

Larry clapped his hands, and the Marlin State team broke from the huddle and lined up.

Larry took the snap and dropped straight back,

cocking his arm and scanning the field. To his left, Eddie Evans, the left end, was loping downfield. Eddie hooked suddenly and stopped, and Larry fired. The ball was on target, but Eddie dropped it. It was a case of trying to turn and start running before he had the ball under control.

Pearce watched the players return to the huddle, and he caught Eddie's eye for a moment when the embarrassed end cast a sad glance at the bench. Pearce nodded slightly. Pearce knew the play Larry would be calling in the huddle. The rule was simple when a receiver dropped a pass on an otherwise perfect play: call the same play again. The strategy gave the erring player a chance to redeem himself, and usually it caught the defense off-balance.

The Tigers broke out of the huddle and lined up.

Larry took the snap and backpedaled quickly, looking over the field. Eddie went downfield and hooked again in the same spot. Winnie the Pooh was running his patented crossing pattern over center, drawing some of the defenders with him. Larry uncorked the pass, and this time Eddie stood there, riveted to the ground, and caught the ball. He was dropped immediately for an eight-yard gain to the Warren Tech forty-seven-yard line. That made it third down and two for a first down.

Larry looked at the bench, but Pearce did not give him any signal. The coach knelt there, chewing his blade of grass and looking for all the world like a casual observer.

Larry knew what to call. They had been over it dozens of times in the past week. The rule was: any time we've got three yards or less to go for a first down, give it to Stetson over right tackle, so Joe Talmadge blocks up front; he's the best we've got.

Larry took the snap, began backpedaling, and handed off to the rushing Louie Stetson—a dangerous way to make a hand-off that most quarterbacks wouldn't dare—and Stetson hit the line behind Talmadge.

The backpedaling maneuver almost fooled the Warren Tech defense, but not quite. The linebacker began to fade, and then changed direction and charged straight for the hole Talmadge was making in the line. The linebacker was there when Louie hit the line, and he got him. It was a one-yard gain, making it fourth down and one yard to go.

Pearce couldn't help feeling a little admiration for the Warren Tech coach. He had done his homework. He knew as well as Pearce that the Tigers' best shot on a short-yardage situation was Stetson running into a hole being opened by Joe Talmadge. The coach had told his linebacker about this play, because the linebacker, after a brief moment of doubt, had charged straight for the hole, even before Larry or Louie had committed himself. That bit of brainwork had saved the situation for Warren Tech, and now Marlin State must kick the ball away.

The Marlin State cheering section was shouting, "Go, go, go."

But this wasn't the time for taking a chance on fourth and one at midfield. Maybe later a gamble would be necessary. But not now. Pearce waved the punter onto the field, and Larry jogged to the sideline.

The spiraling kick backed the Eagles up against their goal, and they started from the twelve-yard line.

Larry pulled on his parka and went over and knelt next to Pearce. "Sorry," he said.

"Not your fault," Pearce said.

"Well, they know now."

"Yep, we haven't got the secret any longer." Pearce looked at the scoreboard, its 7-7 standing out in lights. "And we're starting from even."

chapter 7

The first quarter ended a few minutes later. Pearce got up and walked to the bench and took the headphone from Cody.

"Avery, this is Chuck."

Avery Smith was in the press box, handling the spotting as he had for four years. A bank teller during the week, he became an assistant coach on Saturdays during football season, putting his experience as a Marlin State halfback ten years ago to good use. As a player he had been known as a coach on the field. Now he was a Saturday coach in the press box, sitting with his headset strapped on and a pair of binoculars held in front of his eyes, looking for the signs visible only from above the scene, the small telltale signs that sometimes made all the difference between victory and defeat.

"Two things, Chuck. First, their secondary was all over Louie on that short-yardage plunge. They knew who would get the ball and where he would go, right over Joe Talmadge. Larry's drop-back pattern on the hand-off fooled them for a second, but not enough. And I'll bet it won't come close to fooling them next time. The heck of it is, if Larry had pitched out to his left, we could've scored without a hand being laid on the ball carrier. Everybody was going for Joe Talmadge's slot."

"I know," Chuck said. "What else?"

"We need a keeper play, a quarterback option."

"We can't do that."

"I know, Chuck, but if Larry could just go around end once with the ball, it would keep that secondary honest. They're coming around pretty fast to the idea that Larry isn't going to run the ball. They know that if he holds the ball, he's going to pass, and they react accordingly. They're going to be doing this more and more, and it's going to be murder when they finally decide that they're one hundred percent right about Larry not running with the ball. They'll watch for the hand-off and the pitchout. Larry's got to commit himself pretty quickly on those plays. Then, if he doesn't get rid of the ball, they're going to fall back and cover everything like a blanket."

"That all?"

"One other thing you'll want to pass on to Larry. They're scared to death of Winnie. They're not double-teaming him exactly, but every man in that secondary has got one eye on him. That's how Eddie Evans turned up clear on the same pass play twice in a row. If his defender hadn't been trying to watch Winnie at the same time, we might have had an interception."

"Okay. Thanks, Avery."

"Oh, Chuck."

"Yeah?"

"That kid Larry is just about the best passer I've ever seen. The best this conference has ever seen, no doubt."

"I know it."

"If he'd only run once in a while. . . ."

"I know."

Chuck handed the headphone back to Cody and turned to the field. Warren Tech was coming out of the huddle for a third down and five on its own forty-two-yard line. That was the one blessing of the game, Pearce thought. At least, we're keeping them in their end of the field.

The thought had barely cleared Pearce's mind when the Warren Tech quarterback took the snap and started his turn. Chinigo burst over the line and got one arm on him. His momentum carried him past the quarterback, but the impact of his strong arm sideswiping the quarterback's shoulder knocked off the timing of the play. By the time the quarterback recovered, the halfback who was supposed to receive the hand-off had gone through the line empty-handed.

For a split second the quarterback stood flat-footed and dumbfounded, the ball in his hand and nobody to give it to. Chinigo was recovering and coming back for another shot at him, when the quarterback—on instinct, or blind luck, or whatever—broke to his right.

The line of scrimmage was a jumble of bodies by this time. The blockers up front were as confused as their quarterback. They didn't know which way the play was going. The defense was no better off. At least three of the Marlin State linemen had pummeled the empty-handed halfback coming over guard. Others were caught in the fray and didn't know who had the ball. The men in the secondary spotted the quarterback going to his right, and they saw their own teammates in the line scrambling like blinded elephants. Their instincts sucked them forward and in the direction of the quarterback, now loping, almost in slow motion, toward the sideline.

Suddenly the quarterback stopped, planted his feet, and passed across the field. Marlin State's defensive halfbacks screeched to a halt in horror, wheeled, and began their panicky pursuit of the ball's target, a halfback standing alone on the fifty-yard line.

The pass wasn't a good one. But it didn't have to be good. The ball sailed high in the air, and it wobbled, but that didn't matter. The halfback waited, caught it, and raced fifty yards to the goal untouched.

Pearce was on his feet the moment the quarterback missed his hand-off, knowing that a good team could explode for a touchdown from anywhere on the field in one of those crazy busted plays that leave everybody scattered all over the countryside.

The one hope, Pearce thought, as the Warren Tech halfback crossed the goal, is a penalty for too many men downfield. It frequently happened on a busted play that the linemen, not knowing what was happening, would let themselves roam far beyond the line of scrimmage, hoping to block, only to find themselves declared illegal pass receivers when, in fact, the quarterback had thrown the ball.

Pearce watched and waited for an official to throw a flag. But none did.

The kick made it 14-7.

Pearce scuffed the ground with the toe of his shoe. Two flukes, two touchdowns.

chapter 8

At the half time Pearce and Cody and Avery went over assignments and tried to offer constructive criticism. But what was there to say? Don't fumble? Don't let 'em turn a busted play into a touchdown? Don't drop passes?

Pearce climbed onto a training table in the last few minutes of the intermission.

"Men," he said and looked around the room. There was Chinigo, with dried blood under his nose. There was Louie Stetson, absolutely expressionless, as always. There were Larry Hudson and Harry Willis, sitting together in front of a locker, a study in contrasts, with Harry dirty and bruised from his few plays and Larry unmarked and clean. And there was Winnie, reliving his fumble.

"Men," Pearce said again, "we're going to win this game." He paused. "Oh, sure, the coach is giving a pep talk now. But I mean it. Stop and look at what you've done. You have played those guys off their feet. You're ahead 7-0 if we just count honest touchdowns. You've carried the game to them all the way. We've played ninety percent of the game in their end of the field. We were generous a couple of times, and they got a touchdown out of each of our gifts. Don't be generous in the second half. Keep playing the way you've been playing, and those guys don't have a chance. They know it as well as you. What can they say to themselves in the dressing room right now? Just one thing, and that's that except for a couple of flukes, they'd be a beaten team at this very moment. They know it, and you know. Now let's go out there and prove it."

The players walked out of the dressing room and

down the corridor and broke into a run as they came out from under the stadium.

Chuck Pearce followed them.

The Marlin State kickoff went into the hands of number eighteen, the same halfback who had taken the pass on the busted play for a touchdown. A little guy with speed, he zipped up the center of the field into a crowd of blockers and cut to the sideline. For a terrifying moment, he seemed clear for a touchdown. But Chinigo came out of nowhere and knocked him out of bounds at the Marlin State thirty-yard line.

Three running plays netted eight yards for the Eagles, and they stood on the Marlin State twenty-two-yard line with fourth down and two to go.

Pearce knew what was coming. Warren Tech had a good field-goal kicker, and he trotted onto the field. He did his duty, booting the ball straight and true for three points and a 17-7 Warren Tech lead.

Pearce was on the headphone. "Avery, what happened on that kickoff return?"

"That kid's just fast. He did most of it himself."

Pearce returned to the sidelines, knelt, and plucked a blade of grass. The Tigers were on their own twenty-two-yard line, starting their first series after the kickoff.

Larry took the snap and backpedaled quickly.

Then he stopped, turned to his right and ran, then stopped again, planted his right foot, and let fly with a bomb.

Winnie the Pooh whizzed past midfield and looked back over his left shoulder. The ball was there, high, going over his head. Winnie turned on the speed and took another look. It was coming down, right at him. He crossed the thirty-yard line just as the ball settled into his arms. At the twenty-yard line, he cut slightly to his left, toward the center of the field, and the frantic grasp of a leaping defender dragged across his hips and slid off. Winnie was still on his feet. He cut back to his right and went into the end zone straight-away.

Eddie Evans was the first player to reach Winnie, and he leaped onto him in a bear hug. Louie Stetson was right behind.

Larry jogged off the field, and Mitch Reynolds went in for his automatic kick, 17-14, with Warren Tech out front by three.

Pearce patted Winnie on the rump, clapped Larry on the shoulder, and went to the headphone.

Avery was ecstatic. "That was better than fifty yards in the air," he boomed, "and you could have threaded a needle with it."

"We're not out front yet," Pearce said.

The remainder of the third quarter was fought out between the thirty-yard lines. Larry completed three short passes, two to Eddie Evans on the buttonhook and one to Winnie in the flat, but the Tigers couldn't put a drive together. Larry took another shot at a bomb but overthrew Winnie. Warren Tech stuck to its grinding ground game, pounding the center with the fullback and sending the halfbacks scooting around the ends. But they couldn't sustain a drive either.

At the start of the fourth quarter Warren Tech had the ball on its own thirty-five-yard line. The Eagles wanted a touchdown, but they would have been happy to settle for a scoreless fourth quarter. Most of all right now, they needed to keep possession of the ball. They had seen what Larry Hudson could do in one catastrophic moment with Winnie the Pooh on the receiving end. And they knew that Marlin State could not afford to settle for a scoreless fourth quarter.

Warren Tech's basic strategy remained unchanged, relying on the crunching ground game in the hope that finally they would be able to put together the four-yard gains into a touchdown drive. Even if the strategy didn't get them a touchdown, it would eat up the clock.

Bruno Chinigo danced around behind the line of scrimmage, patting the rumps of the crouching linemen and shouting encouragement in a husky voice that revealed that he was worn to a frazzle. But still, with every snap of the ball to the Warren Tech quarterback, Chinigo sprang into action, charging into the line, weaving his way to the right or left, or dropping back a step to watch and then plunging toward the ball carrier.

In six plays, the rushing machine of Warren Tech had moved through two first downs and twenty-one yards to the Marlin State forty-four-yard line. The clock showed almost five minutes gone, a bare ten minutes left in the game.

The Marlin State cheering section shouted, "Get that ball, get that ball."

Pearce knelt on the sideline, squinting into the setting sun, and thought, Well, they've got the right idea. Get that ball.

Larry stood on the sideline, his hands jammed into the pockets of his parka, waiting.

Warren Tech's big fullback went through the center of the line and, with Chinigo cut down by a vicious block, rambled through to the twenty-five-yard line. A defensive halfback, Charley Frost, fought off a blocker and pulled him down there. Chinigo, back on his feet, was coming in fast and piled into the falling fullback, and the ball squirted free.

A cloud of jerseys swarmed over the ball at the twenty-four-yard line.

Pearce stood up. Larry stepped forward and peered at the pile of players on the field. There was a tense silence as the referee picked his way through the tangle of bodies.

Then there was a roar from the Marlin State cheering section as the referee flexed his arm and pointed to the Warren Tech goal—Marlin State's ball!

Charley Frost, the defensive halfback who had made the tackle, was the last man up. He ran to the sideline with a smile spread across his face and his arms held up, fists clenched, as Larry tossed his parka onto the bench and jogged onto the field with the offense unit.

Pearce looked at the clock. Nine minutes and twenty seconds. And seventy-six yards. "Plenty of time," he shouted to Larry.

Larry nodded.

Larry pitched out to Winnie for six yards, handed off to Louie for three yards, and pitched out to Burlington for four yards around left end and a first down on the Marlin State thirty-seven-yard line.

Warren Tech's defense was watching for the pass,

either the long bomb to Winnie or the buttonhook to Eddie Evans, and the runners were getting the split second they needed for a half-step advantage.

Pearce knelt at the sideline watching. The sequence of plays Larry was calling had been pounded out in those sessions around Pearce's dining table. "The march to the sea," Pearce had called it, the special series of plays designed for just such an occasion —the last long charge for a touchdown—with Larry using the threat of the pass as effectively as he used the pass itself.

Now the second series began, with the Warren Tech defense a little uncertain.

Larry took the snap and backpedaled, faking to Stetson plunging into the middle of the line, and zipped a bullet pass to Johnson at the sideline. It was worth eight yards and stopped the clock when Johnson stepped out of bounds.

The next play was identical, except Larry gave the ball to Stetson this time for a plunge over Joe Talmadge's tackle position. Louie got the two yards needed for a first down, plus one, to put the ball on the forty-eight.

A pass to Eddie Evans on the buttonhook crossed the fifty-yard line and carried to the Warren Tech forty-five-yard line, a seven-yard gain. And a bullet to Winnie on the sideline gained seven more to the Warren Tech thirty-eight-yard line. Warren Tech called time out.

Larry jogged to the sideline where Pearce was standing.

"Avery says the runs and the short passes are sucking them in pretty good," Pearce said. "Try the bellringer to Winnie." The bellringer was the long bomb.

Larry nodded and returned to the huddle.

Taking the snap from center, Larry backpedaled, turned to his right and ran, then stopped and planted his foot. Winnie was already inside the ten-yard line and looking back over his left shoulder.

Out of nowhere, from his blind side, a Warren Tech lineman grazed Larry with a glancing blow. Larry had just completed his turn to plant his foot, and the charging lineman didn't have time to change direction with his moving target. The lineman fell on past Larry.

Momentarily off balance, Larry began moving away from the point of impact. He was looking downfield, trying to locate Winnie again for the long pass. Cocking his arm as he ran, Larry now had Winnie in his sights, circling near the goal.

To Larry's left, another lineman was zeroing in on him.

From the sideline, Pearce could not tell whether

Larry was aware of the tackler storming in from his blind side. Then Larry glanced quickly over his shoulder at the lineman rocketing in toward him.

"Scramble," Pearce involuntarily said aloud. Larry would have to twist out of the tackler's reach and then pass to Winnie the Pooh. Or, if the scrambling left him out of position for the long throw to the goal, he could release the ball to his safety-valve receiver, Burlington T. Johnson, circling near the sideline.

But Larry didn't scramble. He dropped to one knee and downed the ball on the Warren Tech forty-eight-yard line. The startled Warren Tech lineman veered at the last moment to avoid crashing into the downed quarterback.

Pearce stared at the scene on the field. Larry remained down on one knee for what seemed like ages. Finally he got to his feet. In front of him was Louie Stetson, who had tried to block the charging Warren Tech lineman. The big fullback never changed his expression, and he didn't do it now. But Pearce had no doubt as to what was in Louie's mind. Off to the right, Burlington T. Johnson was staring at Larry open-mouthed. Winnie the Pooh jogged into the scene. He was wearing a puzzled expression.

Cody appeared beside Pearce. "We've got to pull him out," he said.

"No," Pearce said. He looked onto the field, and for

a moment his eyes met Larry's. Then Larry looked away.

The referee was calling the resumption of play.

Larry did not look at the players in the huddle. He called the play and broke the huddle. He didn't clap his hands this time.

First down and twenty yards to go on the forty-eight-yard line, with the clock showing a few seconds over six minutes remaining in the game.

Larry took the snap, straightened up, and fired a bullet to Eddie Evans, racing across the field five yards past the line of scrimmage. Eddie held on, and the play got seven yards.

Larry overshot Johnson, but then a pass to a diving Winnie at the sideline netted twelve yards and a throw to Eddie Evans at the other sideline got ten yards for a first down on the Warren Tech nineteen-yard line with four minutes remaining.

At this point, the script drafted by Pearce called for Larry to signal two plays in the huddle, allowing the Tigers to line up quickly for the second play, perhaps catching the defenders unready.

The first play was a straight hand-off to Louie Stetson. It worked. The change of pace caught the Warren Tech players fluttering all over the field looking for a pass. And while the defenders fluttered,

Louie stormed through the hole opened in the line by Joe Talmadge, nine yards to the ten-yard line.

Lining up without a huddle, the Tigers caught Warren Tech's defenders still scrambling for position as they got their play under way. Larry took the snap on a short signal count and handed off to Burlington T. Johnson, who charged off tackle and gained two yards in a crowd of defenders for a first down on the Warren Tech eight-yard line.

The first down stopped the clock at three minutes and nine seconds remaining. On both sides of the field, players were standing along the sideline.

Pearce stood with his hands on his hips, watching the scene, as the Warren Tech defense dug in to guard the last eight yards to the goal. The Tigers came out of the huddle and lined up.

The grandstands on both sides of the field were bedlam. The Warren Tech fans were screaming, "Throw 'em back, throw 'em back." The Marlin State fans were shouting, "Go, go, go," at the top of their lungs.

Larry moved into position behind the center, looked up and down the line, and barked the signals above the roar of the crowd. He took the snap, dropped straight back quickly, and zipped a bullet pass to Winnie in the corner at the goal line. Winnie leaped and speared the ball and landed out of bounds. The referee ruled Winnie out of bounds when he gained possession of the ball and brought the ball back to the eight-yard-line.

Second down and eight yards for a touchdown.

The Tigers lined up without a huddle for the second play in the sequence, a quick hand-off to Burlington T. Johnson through the middle, designed to take advantage of a defense spread for another pass attempt. But the Warren Tech line held. Johnson barely made one yard.

Third down and seven yards for a touchdown.

Larry took hardly a second in the huddle to call the next two plays. Everybody knew what was coming. It was all written down in the playbook.

Taking the snap, Larry backpedaled quickly, glancing to his left and faking a pass to Eddie Evans, and then fired across field to Winnie in the flat. The fake succeeded in pulling the Warren Tech defenders off-balance for a fraction of a second. And Winnie, with his tremendous speed, was past the line of scrimmage before they recovered.

Winnie raced down the sideline and cut suddenly inside to avoid a defensive halfback coming up fast. Caught at the five, he wiggled and squirmed and fought his way to the one-yard line.

The clock didn't matter now. It was fourth down. The whole game, and maybe the whole season, boiled down to one play and one yard to gain—the toughest yard on any football field, the last yard to the goal. A field goal to tie and a touchdown to win.

Larry looked to the sideline.

Pearce stood there, unmoving, hands on hips. Sure, Mitch Reynolds would never miss a field goal from this distance. But Pearce gave no indication that Larry should do anything other than call the next play for a touchdown.

The referee whistled the play into action. Larry took the snap, stepped back, turned, and handed off to Louie Stetson behind the charging form of Joe Talmadge. The whole world turned into a pile of football players on the goal line as Larry backpedaled from the action and Louie charged into the crowd.

After an interminable wait, the referee's arms shot skyward—touchdown!

Mitch Reynolds' kick for the extra point, even though not needed, was good—21 to 17.

chapter 9

The dressing room was a wild and crazy and happy place, with the jubilation of the victory overshadowing the episode that almost cost the Tigers the game—Larry's shocking decision to go to one knee and take a ten-yard loss instead of scrambling to keep alive the march that was their last hope.

For once Louie Stetson changed expression, beaming a big smile as his teammates swarmed around him with congratulations for scoring the winning touchdown.

Bruno Chinigo, whose refusal to quit on defense had made the victory possible, shouted a battle cry at the top of his lungs, with one arm raised, fist clenched. Charley Frost, whose fumble recovery had opened the way to the winning drive, was standing on a bench, stark naked, shouting, "Whoopee," over and over. Harry Willis, who'd never got back into the game after the few moments of action in the first quarter, was running around the room congratulating everyone he could find.

Harry bounced up to Larry. "Great game, Larry. Just great, really. Great passing."

"Thanks, Harry. We won, and that's what's important."

"Larry," Harry said, "I just want you to know, there's no bad feeling about your getting the call at quarterback. I can't play in your league. You're the best thing that could've happened to the Tigers, and I want you to know that I feel that way."

"Thanks, Harry," Larry said. "I really appreciate that."

Harry moved on to congratulate somebody else.

Chuck Pearce moved away from the celebration

and stepped into the coaches' dressing room, taking a seat on the edge of a table, his shoulders slumped forward.

"You should be a happy man," said Bill Oliver, sticking his head inside the door.

"Yep," Pearce said and nodded. "Winning feels better than losing, every time."

Avery was seated on a bench in front of a locker, leaning back and holding one knee clasped in his hands.

Cody was already out of the shower and dressing himself.

"Now that we've got the congratulations out of the way. . . ." Oliver said, his voice trailing off.

"Yeah, I know, Bill," Pearce said.

"Your secret is out of the bag now."

"Yeah, I know."

Avery interjected with, "That boy completed sixteen of twenty-one passes. Should've been seventeen, if Eddie hadn't dropped that easy buttonhook in the first quarter."

Pearce looked at Avery and then at Bill Oliver, and the bespectacled sports editor returned his gaze. "Yeah, Avery," Pearce said, "but that isn't what Bill is talking about."

"I mean you had another secret, and it's out now," Oliver said.

"How's that?"

"What are you going to do with a great passer who puts his knee to the ground the first time it looks like somebody is going to hit him?"

"I thought that's what you were talking about," Pearce said.

"Aw, hell," Avery interrupted. "The kid who won the game made one mistake along the way, and all you guys want to talk about is that one mistake. You make me sick."

"Is he scared of getting hit?" Oliver asked.

"You writing a story?" Pearce asked.

"That's my job."

"Okay, for your story, I'll tell you something," Pearce said. "Larry Hudson is the greatest passer the SIAA has ever seen. He's on this football team with simple instructions from me—stay healthy and keep throwing. What the hell good is he to us on the bench with a shoulder separation? Or with torn ligaments in his knee? I'll give up five or ten yards that he might make by scrambling in return for the passes he delivers any time at all. Any time at all."

Pearce paused while Oliver scribbled in his notebook.

"And one more thing," he said. "You know what I found out on that field today? I found out that our team is just as good as Warren Tech without Larry

Hudson. Just as good, but not better. Do you understand? With Larry Hudson, we were better. He was the difference out there. I want the man who is the difference to stay healthy."

"I'm quoting you, okay?"

"Please do."

Bill Oliver continued to scribble for a few moments, then leaned back, lit a cigarette, smiled, and said, "And now, Coach, about today's game."

Pearce laughed. Oliver had been too good a friend during Pearce's six years at the helm of the Marlin State football team for the touching of a nerve to end it all. But he had indeed touched a nerve.

Pearce started to rehash the game, commenting on the strategies he had used, when a second reporter, Henry Edmonds of the *Warren Courier*, walked in.

The thought occurred to Pearce that Oliver really had been a friend, getting the question of Larry Hudson's dropping to his knee out of the way before other reporters made their way into the dressing room.

The dressing room was almost empty when Pearce, alone, walked to the showers. The players had gone, some of them already on their way back to Marlin in friends' cars, some of them milling around waiting for the bus to leave. Cody was going with the bus, so they didn't have to wait for Pearce, and he enjoyed the slow shower.

The sportswriters had come and gone, and they were upstairs in the press box now writing their stories about what the coaches had to say. They were busy making a hero out of Larry Hudson, no doubt.

Pearce wasn't smiling as he lathered and rinsed in the shower. He thought that he should have been smiling. His team had knocked off the odds-on favorite for the conference championship. Nobody else on the schedule should be as tough as Warren Tech. The Warren Tech coach had told him at midfield after the game, "You've got a winner there, Chuck." The *Warren Courier* sportswriter had told him, "Looks like clear sailing to the title." But Chuck Pearce knew that, no matter what, the schedule had nine games on it, and only two had been played. The Tigers might look unbeatable today. But the Warren Tech Eagles had looked unbeatable yesterday, and look at what had happened to them.

Pearce stepped out of the shower and began drying himself. "Quit kidding yourself," he muttered. "You've got a powerhouse, but it's got a powder keg sitting right in the middle of it with a short fuse."

He had seen Larry Hudson drop to one knee when it looked as if he was going to be tackled. Everybody had seen that. But Pearce's practiced eye had seen other things, too, and some of them were even more frightening. He had seen the wind go out of Louie

Stetson when Louie realized what Larry had done and why. And Pearce had, just by luck, a straight look into the huddle once when Larry came into it and told Winnie, "Bad pass, my fault," and he had seen Winnie's glare from under the brow of his helmet. He had seen, through the pane of glass separating the coaches' dressing room from the players' dressing room, Larry Hudson standing apart, unnoticed and quiet, in the midst of the jubilation. By all rights, Larry should have been the hero raised to the heights by the team.

And he didn't look forward to rallying the practice session on Monday, with the new hero wearing sweat clothes and throwing passes to Byron Farr down behind the goalposts.

Pearce knotted his tie in place, pulled on his sports jacket, and walked out of the dressing room to find Maggie waiting in the corridor.

"Sorry I was so long, honey," he said.

"That's okay. Want to eat at Bearden's?"

"Sure, sounds fine."

As they walked to the car, Maggie said, "Why did he go down on his knee?"

Pearce stopped in his tracks and looked at his wife. "You, too!" he bellowed, and laughed.

chapter 10

At six o'clock the next morning, Sunday, Chuck Pearce was putting the key in the front door of the field house and opening the door, as he did every Sunday morning during football season.

Downstairs in the projection room just off Pearce's office, Jerry Phillips, the student manager, was already there, putting the reel of film in place and getting the film threaded. "This one's going to be fun to watch, Coach," Jerry said.

"You bet," said Pearce and walked into his office to await Cody and Avery. Jerry had plugged in the coffee pot, and Pearce helped himself to a cup.

They were an hour into the filming—the stop, backup, restart, stop, with comments and notes, studying every player's performance on every play—when the door in the projection room opened. Pearce could see the outline of Larry Hudson in the light from beyond.

"Mind?" Larry asked.

"No, of course not," Pearce said.

They went ahead with the work until they reached the half time

"Let's take the intermission," Pearce said. "I could use a cup of coffee. Helluva game Chinigo played, wasn't it?"

"Helluva game," Cody agreed.

Larry followed Pearce into his office. "Could I speak with you a minute, Coach, in private?"

"Sure," Pearce said and closed the door.

"Have you seen the papers?"

"No, I haven't," Pearce said.

"It seems I'm a miracle man," Larry said, shrugging his shoulders and laughing slightly.

"Oh?"

"Only I'm not, of course."

"No, of course you're not," Pearce said. "None of us ever is."

Larry took a seat on the straight-back chair, and Pearce leaned against the desk. "What's on your mind, Larry?"

"You know what's on my mind," Larry said. "I think that I should quit. I think I never should've gotten myself—and you—into this. I should've known it would never work. Never. Not ever."

"And so you want to quit, now that you're a miracle man?" Pearce tried to speak gently. He hoped to jolt Larry without shattering him.

Larry looked at him for a moment. "I was afraid. That's why I put my knee down. I was afraid."

"I know that."

"Is that all you've got to say?" Larry asked.

"Well, I'll say that I wasn't surprised. You'd told me that you were afraid of getting hurt. I believed you. I assumed all along you'd do anything to keep from getting hit. So I wasn't surprised."

Larry was seated, hunched forward, his elbows on his knees. As Pearce spoke, Larry gazed at the floor. He seemed not to be listening. Pearce had the feeling that Larry's mind was miles away, dwelling on something else, and that Larry was wondering whether he should tell the coach everything that was on his mind. Pearce sat without speaking, waiting.

"Coach," Larry said finally, "maybe I ought to tell you. . . ."

"If you want to," Pearce said.

Larry looked at the coach. "You never heard of Brad Hudson," he said.

Pearce said nothing but shook his head slowly, his eyes fixed on Larry, waiting for him to continue.

"He's my brother, my older brother."

"Yes. . .?"

"He was a football player, a running back," Larry said and paused, obviously finding the telling painful. "He was great. When he graduated from high school, the big schools from all over the country wanted him. We had a regular parade of coaches through the house that spring. He chose Southern Cal. That was where Dad had played football. So Brad went out to Southern Cal. He made the starting lineup as a freshman. Then he. . . ."

Larry paused, and Pearce watched him closely.

"Then in his sophomore year he was hurt, in the third game, against Oregon," Larry said. "It wasn't the kind of play that is supposed to hurt anybody. He just got knocked out of bounds on an end sweep. But something happened . . . he just got hit the wrong way . . . just the wrong way. . . ."

"I see," Pearce said softly. "And was it bad?"

"His back was injured. His legs were paralyzed. The doctors said he would never walk again." Larry looked at the coach. "He did learn to walk on crutches, finally. He uses them now. You wouldn't know it, to see him sitting at his desk in the bank in Minneapolis where he works. But then he gets up to walk—and those crutches."

"I understand," Pearce said.

Pearce didn't tell Larry, but he recalled the Brad Hudson story now that Larry told him. He remembered reading in the papers—when was it, four or five years ago?—about the injury of the outstanding running back Brad Hudson, who had been expected to have a sensational career. Pearce thought he should have tied the two together, both of the Hudsons, before Larry told him the story. But it all happened many miles away from Indiana, and in a football world—the big time of Southern Cal—far removed from the SIAA and Marlin State. Brad Hudson had faded out of the headlines as quickly as he had entered.

"And?" Pearce asked, prompting Larry to continue.

"I was playing high-school ball," Larry said. "And

suddenly all that I could see when I carried the ball was the vision of Brad in that hospital bed, and then in that wheelchair, and then on crutches. I managed to finish the season, but I decided never to play again."

Larry shrugged slightly and gave a small smile. "I did go on and enroll at Southern Cal," he said. "My father had played there. And so had Brad. I know that Brad was hoping I would get over the effects of his injury and would continue the tradition, playing for Southern Cal. Brad felt really strongly about football. But I knew that I had decided never to play again. Finally, I pulled out of Southern Cal. I was through with all of that. I came here. And then that day you. . . ."

Pearce leaned back and folded his arms and studied Larry as the lad let the words trail off into silence.

Pearce had known instinctively from the beginning that there was a story behind Larry's fear. Nobody with Larry's obvious talents and experience as a quarterback suddenly turns up frightened by the game without a reason. Pearce had been confident that the reason would emerge at a time of Larry's choosing. And now here it was—and Pearce had to acknowledge that it was a good one. Larry had seen his brother's promising career and part of his life shattered by an injury on the football field.

Pearce considered the facts rapidly. He started at one point to tell Larry, Okay, you'd better quit. Pearce knew from his own years of experience, both as player and coach, that a frightened player is most apt of all to be injured. And if Larry couldn't whip his fear, the chances were good that he would get hit, and hurt.

Pearce knew without asking that the other players didn't know the story of Brad Hudson, or it had slipped from memory. And Larry certainly hadn't told anyone. Being afraid, and having your teammates know it, would be bad enough. But making excuses with the story of your brother's injury would be even worse.

In the long run, Pearce reflected, the question of the good of the team didn't matter as much as the question of whether Larry Hudson could—or should—defeat his fear.

The coach made his decision and, trying not to look as if he had doubts, leaned forward over the desk and stared intently at Larry. "You wanted to play," he said. "I sensed that on the practice field the first day we met."

"Yes, and I thought—"

"You thought that maybe the old fear was gone. But now you've found that it isn't gone at all. Right?"

"Yes, that's right."

"And so now you want to quit. You figure that you've given it another try, and it didn't work, and that's not your fault; you tried, and now you want to quit."

Larry returned Pearce's gaze. "I don't see any other way."

Pearce waited.

"Did you see Louie Stetson?" Larry asked.

"Yes, I saw him, and I know Louie well enough to know what he was thinking."

"And Winnie. . . ."

"I saw a little of that too."

Larry didn't say anything.

"Are you waiting for me to tell you that I'm throwing you off the team, so you won't have to make the decision for yourself? Are you waiting for me to explain that it's my fault and not your fault that we've got this problem? Are you waiting for me to tell you that you warned me in advance, and that I, as the coach, should've known better? Are you waiting for me to tell you that your continued presence on the squad is going to wreck the morale and shatter the team? Are you waiting for all of that from me?"

"No . . . I mean, I don't know." Larry paused. "I can't look at those guys again." Larry stood up, as if to go.

"Sit back down," Pearce said. "We're not through."

Larry stood a moment, looking at the coach, then sat back down.

"You quit out there on the field, in front of your team and in front of the crowd," Pearce said. "No doubt about that. It's a fact, and it can't be erased. But you should understand that you came back after quitting. With all the pressure, and there was plenty of it, I know, you came back. You took the team down the field, and you won the game. You know it and I know it and every man on the team knows. Sure, the players know that you quit in the clutch when you thought you were going to be hit. But they also know that you came back. Believe me, it'll dawn on them that that is exactly what happened out there. But now, if you quit today, you can't come back in your own eyes. There is no coming back from walking out on this team right now. Sure, you can go. You can quit. But I'm not going to do you the favor of kicking you off the team, so you can blame me for the rest of your life. Quit if you like, but remember that you've got to blame yourself and not me."

Pearce walked around Larry and opened the door. "Now I've got to get back to the film room," he said.

It was almost noon when Pearce and Cody and Avery finished viewing the films and making their notes and trying to analyze every important happening in the game. They moved into Pearce's office, dragging a third chair behind them, and uncovered a tray of sandwiches Maggie had brought by late in the morning.

"Hudson's even better than I thought," Avery said, reflecting on the game films he had just seen.

"Yeah, he is, isn't he?"

"According to my figures," Avery said, "he came within a whisker of completing twenty-one of twenty-one passes, and that's fantastic. If Eddie hadn't dropped that buttonhook pass. . . . If Winnie hadn't broken stride on one of those long bombs. . . . If Winnie had kept his feet in bounds down there in the corner. . . . And do you know what's left? A bullet pass that was off the target, that's what. And it wasn't that much off target. An outstanding receiver would have had it."

Pearce looked at Avery. "Do you think that will make them accept him?"

"He sat by himself on the bus coming back," Cody said.

"He just won't run with the ball, huh?" Avery asked.

"Nope," Pearce said. "He won't run, and that's the deal I made with him."

There was a moment of silence. Cody and Avery

clearly were waiting for Pearce to go on, to tell them something that would explain and justify the unusual arrangement. But Pearce said nothing more.

Pearce had mulled over the benefits of telling Cody and Avery the story of Brad Hudson. He hardly had been able to keep his mind on the films of the second half. They, too, had failed to connect the Brad Hudson story with Larry Hudson's fears. Maybe they had never heard the story of Brad Hudson. Or, if they had heard it, they weren't linking the incident to the Larry Hudson who was playing quarterback for Marlin State.

Telling them now would perhaps make them as understanding of Larry's problem as Pearce was. But Pearce decided against it. First, Larry had spoken to him in confidence, and the coach would keep the player's confidence. And second, Pearce knew that if Larry ever were to whip his problem, he would have to do it himself, without being treated with sympathy and understanding. In the wrong situation, sympathy and understanding could be crutches more restrictive than those used by Brad Hudson.

"How about laying the cards on the table with the team?" Cody asked. "He's scared to run, but he knows he's afraid of being hit. And everybody knows that's that."

"The cards are already on the table," Pearce said.

"Everybody knows he's a great passer. Everybody knows he's afraid of being hit. And everybody knows that I'll accept things on those terms. No, the cards already are on the table."

"The only question now, I guess," Cody said, "is to see how Louie and Bruno and the rest of them decide to play the cards, huh?"

"More than that," Pearce said. "We've also got to see how Larry Hudson is going to play those cards."

chapter 11

Long after Cody and Avery had left the field house and Jerry Phillips had filed away the game films, Chuck Pearce sat in his tiny office alone, with one hand on the telephone on his desk.

He picked up the telephone and dialed the long-distance operator.

"The residence of Brad Hudson, in Minneapolis, or

maybe St. Paul," he said. "I don't have the number."

A few moments later, Pearce was listening to a robust voice saying, "Yes, this is Brad Hudson."

From the sound of the voice, Pearce found it difficult to imagine Brad Hudson crippled for life and hobbling on crutches. He could tell, without ever having met Brad Hudson, why Larry would consider his brother's accident such a tragedy.

"My name is Chuck Pearce, and I'm the football coach at Marlin State in Indiana."

"Yes?"

"Did you know that your brother, Larry, is playing football for me?"

There was a long pause, during which Pearce felt a multitude of doubts sweeping over him. With Larry so clearly trying to defeat his fears alone, he knew that the announcement must be coming as news to Brad Hudson. Pearce had no way of knowing how Brad might react, with the memory of his own injury living with him every day on crutches. Brad could easily view Larry's playing with horror. He undoubtedly knew of Larry's fears, and there was a chance he might be sharing the fears. There was a chance that Brad Hudson, on his crutches, held nothing but bitterness for the sport that had promised him so much and then robbed him of so much. Because of the fears, or the bitterness, he might oppose the idea of Larry's playing. Or, perhaps worst of all, he might object when he learned of the hard line that Pearce had taken with Larry, trying to force him to face up to his fear. There were dangers for Larry in the move, Pearce knew, and Brad Hudson would know also. There was no saying in advance how Brad would react, but Pearce felt he had to tell Larry's brother and, if possible, obtain his counsel.

"Well, I'll be darned," the voice of Brad Hudson boomed over the telephone line. Pearce thought he could hear a smile behind the voice. "That's great news, really great."

Pearce sighed in relief, then took a deep breath and plunged ahead. "It's not all roses really, and that's why I'm calling you," he said.

"Oh?"

Pearce filled in Brad on the background: the first pass he had seen Larry throw on the practice field, the conversations about Larry's coming out for the team and Larry's fears, the special arrangement they had agreed on, the other players' feelings, and, finally, the incident in the Warren Tech game when Larry went to his knee and took a loss to avoid getting hit.

"I see," Brad Hudson said, when Pearce finished.

"He's pretty upset, and he tried to quit the team this morning. That was when he told me about you and about your being the reason for his fears."

"And?"

"Frankly, I was pretty rough on him," Pearce said. "I told him that if he quit now he would have to face the fact for the rest of his life that he was a quitter. I told him that he would have to figure out for himself what to do, whether he wanted to stick it out now and defeat his fear, or whether he wanted to surrender to his fear."

"What did he say?"

"Well, nothing, really, and that's where we left it. I don't know what he's going to do. I doubt if he knows himself at the present time."

Brad Hudson said nothing for a moment, then asked, "You want him to continue playing?"

"I think that is the important thing for Larry right now," Pearce said.

"I appreciate your looking at it that way, Coach, but what I meant was, What about your team—the morale, the attitude—in this kind of a situation? I was a player, and I know what this kind of thing can do."

Pearce knew too that doubts and dissension could wreck a good team. He had wondered with a twinge of conscience, when he threw the challenge at Larry a few hours ago, if his prime concern was Larry or the team's need for a standout passer. He had brooded over this point before calling Brad Hudson, and he suspected now that that was really what was behind Brad's question.

"Brad," he said, choosing his words carefully, "I'm looking at it this way: if Larry overcomes his fears, that will be great for Larry and great for the team; if he stays and remains too scared to look at himself in the mirror, or if he ducks out and quits, well, either one would be a tragedy for Larry and also a tragedy for the team. So you can see, on every count, what's good for Larry and what's good for the team are going hand in hand."

"Yes," Brad said. And then he asked, "What do you want me to do?"

"I don't think there is anything for you to do at the moment," Pearce said. "Or for me to do either. It's up to Larry at this point. But I thought that you should know, and I want to say that I certainly would be willing to listen to any advice about what's the best thing for Larry. It seems to me that he's got to overcome this fear while he has the chance."

"I agree with that," Brad said. "I've known about his problem, of course. He played out his junior year in high school and quit. He could have followed in my footsteps—and our father's footsteps—playing at Southern Cal. He was that good. I guess you know that by now. He did attend Southern Cal for a year, and, well, I was hoping he would pick up a football. But he always said he wasn't interested in playing anymore; that it wasn't worth it to him. I knew, though, that it was important to him. It was a sad thing to watch."

"I'm afraid it will become even sadder as the years pass for him," Pearce said.

Brad was quiet a moment, and then said, "You have a game this week, I guess."

"Yes, Brenway College. They haven't got much. It should be an easy one. Larry won't be needed often and probably won't play a lot. He shouldn't have any trouble living with his fears through the Brenway game. But the following week—well, that's another story. It's Oakman State. They're pretty tough. The team will need Larry, and Larry knows it."

"Well, Coach, I'm on your side. But I don't think I should get into the act right now. Larry didn't tell me that he was going out for football, and maybe that is significant. I guess he had his reasons, and we should respect them."

"I agree."

"For what it's worth, I'm behind you, Coach Pearce. Let me know if I can help."

"I certainly will," Pearce said. "And I appreciate your attitude."

"Keep me posted."

"You bet."

Pearce hung up the telephone. Brad Hudson sounded to him like a helluva guy. And Pearce decided that Brad's younger brother, Larry, probably was made of the same stuff. But Larry was facing a sterner challenge than even Brad with his injury had seen in his playing days. And the question of whether Larry would face up to the challenge remained to be answered.

Pearce closed up the office and headed for home.

chapter 12

Chuck Pearce arrived at his office in the field house early on Monday and dug into his usual routine, reviewing his notes on last Saturday's game films to discuss with the team and laying out his week's plan for practice. His goal was to keep the players' eyes on the Brenway College game but at the same time use some of the practice week to polish special strategy for use the following week against the tougher Oakman State.

Although Pearce didn't tell anyone, he was prepared to meet the Monday afternoon practice session with Larry Hudson missing—perhaps for good.

Pearce had intentionally terminated the conversation with Larry without demanding an immediate answer: stick it out or quit. In fact, he had steered the conversation toward its finish in such a way that Larry couldn't announce a final decision, even if that was what he thought he wanted to do. Pearce figured the young quarterback needed time to reach the right decision. And he was satisfied he had put Larry in the position of having to take time to make the decision, rather than blurting out his first reaction, which certainly would have been to quit. Maybe time would change his mind.

If Larry failed to appear for practice today, Pearce would make excuses and then, like it or not, he would have to press for an answer on Tuesday. After all, Larry's absence one day wouldn't disrupt practice, even though he had a key position as quarterback. For Larry, practice was mostly throwing passes down behind the goalposts to Byron Farr while Harry Willis directed the offense. The other parts of Larry's practicing involved hand-offs, pitchouts, and passes with the first-string offense, solely to get everyone accustomed to the timing. And with Larry, this never was a problem.

Pearce sighed as he reflected that even if Larry Hudson decided to stay with the team, the problem of the other players was still with them and probably would get worse before it got better.

"One problem at a time," he reminded himself.

Late in the morning, as Pearce was completing his notes and stacking them for the clipboard he always carried on the practice field, Larry appeared in his office door.

"Coach?" he asked tentatively.

Pearce looked up. "Come in, Larry."

"Do you have a minute?"

"Of course. Have a seat."

Larry placed his books on the edge of Pearce's desk and sat on the wooden chair facing the coach. "You said I'd be sorry if I quit," Larry said.

Pearce nodded slightly but said nothing, waiting for Larry to continue.

"Does that mean that you want me to stay on the team . . . this way?"

Pearce studied Larry's handsome face. It was a troubled face. Pearce could imagine what was going on in Larry's mind. The coach had hoped for the most, that Larry would come in and announce that he would be a full-time quarterback and run the ball, in a determined effort to defeat his fears once and for all. But Larry wasn't saying that. His troubled face indicated that he wanted to say it, but he wasn't ready.

"Larry, we made a deal on that first day, and I'm willing to stick by it, if you are."

"If you'll have me, I want to stay."

"I think you're making the right decision."

Larry said nothing for a moment, then spoke as if he had not heard what Pearce said. "I can't get out of my mind the way Louie and Winnie and the rest of them looked at me."

"You can overcome that," Pearce said.

Pearce wanted to add that one end run would solve the problem. But he held back in the belief that Larry would have to advance one step at a time, and returning to face the team in practice this afternoon—even under the condition that he wouldn't run—would be the first big step.

Larry stood up. "Well, I thought I ought to come in and . . . ."

"Sure," Pearce said. "I'm glad you did. I'll see you at practice."

Larry nodded and left.

Pearce had barely settled back in his chair when the telephone rang. The caller was Henry Osgood.

"Chuck," he said, "you're going to have that boy, Larry Hudson, at the luncheon today, aren't you?"

The alumni luncheon was held each Monday during the football season. Pearce always attended to review the previous week's game and discuss the upcoming opponent. He usually took along two or three players. The alumni enjoyed meeting them, and the players viewed an invitation to join their coach at the head table as a sort of reward for a game well played.

"I had planned on bringing Winnie and Bruno," Pearce said. And then he quickly added "But, yes, of course, I'll have Larry with me too."

"Just thought I'd check and be sure," Osgood said. "Some of the members have already asked me if he will be there."

"He will," Pearce said and hung up the telephone.

Pearce leaned back in his chair and sighed. He could not help smiling at his good fortune that Henry Osgood had not dialed him a half hour earlier. At that time, Pearce had not known whether Larry Hudson even was a member of the Marlin State football team. He mused about the reaction if he had had to announce at the alumni luncheon that Larry Hudson, star passer, had quit the team. "They would probably lynch me on the spot," he said aloud.

He was still smiling when he got up and walked out of his office to send a message to Larry in the classroom about joining him, along with Bruno and Winnie, at the alumni luncheon.

But Pearce's good spirits were short-lived. When he and the players met for the short drive into town, Winnie pointedly failed even to say hello to Larry. And Bruno gave Larry only the slightest of nods.

The four of them should have been happy and confident. They had just whipped Warren Tech, the leading contender for the SIAA championship, in a magnificent come-from-behind rally. They had discovered an ace passer. They were undefeated so far in the young season, and they had the easy Brenway College team coming up this week.

Pearce was scowling as he drove away. His worst imaginings about the team's reaction to Larry's fear were coming true.

Larry, in the back seat, tried to strike up a conversation with Bruno. "I was at the field house on Sunday morning when the coaches were running the films, and I got to see you catch that number eighteen from behind," he said. "That was some play. He was gone for a touchdown until you nailed him. Even in the films, I don't see how you did it."

Bruno was only human, and the words of praise

struck a receptive chord with him. After all, defensive players find rave notices pretty few and far between, despite the beating they take. And, for Bruno, receiving the praise from the game's acknowledged hero was something extra. "Well, thanks," Bruno said, sounding a little embarrassed.

Winnie turned in the front seat and glared straight into Hudson's eyes. "You mean you wanted to see the game films?"

Pearce winced and tried to look at Larry in the rear-view mirror, but Larry was leaning back into a corner and was out of the range of vision.

"I didn't go to the field house to see the films," Larry said. "But the coaches were running them when I was there, and I saw some of the action."

Winnie turned back to the front and didn't reply. The rest of the ride was silent, and Pearce thanked his lucky stars the drive was such a short one in the small town of Marlin.

The usual procedure at the football luncheon was for Pearce to introduce the players he had brought along, with a few words explaining their importance in last Saturday's game, and then to discuss the game, putting the emphasis on the roles played by the young men at the head table with him.

He introduced Bruno as the "only linebacker in the

world who can outrun the fastest halfback that Warren Tech has." And everybody, knowing the play that Pearce was referring to, applauded and cheered while Bruno took a little bow.

Pearce described Winnie as a "man whose mother calls him Winston, but we call him Winnie the Pooh, and Warren Tech calls him absolute murder." Everybody applauded and cheered, and Winnie stood up and gave a little wave and sat back down.

Pearce turned to Larry and, in a brief instant, got the uneasy feeling that the room was too quiet. It was as if this was what everyone had come for, the main event, and that Bruno and Winnie had been just the preliminaries. "This next man I'm going to introduce is new to you," Pearce said. "This is his first year at Marlin State, and he's played only one game. But you all know by now—and so does Warren Tech—that he is able to pass a football. Larry Hudson."

Larry half rose from his chair and nodded, and the applause started. Then Henry Osgood, at the head table, got to his feet and held his hands high, clapping them together in a signal for others in the room to get to their feet. In a moment, the audience of fifty men was standing and applauding.

Larry flushed and cast a plaintive look at Pearce.

Pearce didn't have to look at Winnie. He could

imagine the expression on his face. Never in his six years of introducing players at the alumni-association football luncheons had Pearce seen the audience get to its feet for a standing ovation for one player. It should have been a good moment, but all that Pearce could think about was what would happen at practice this afternoon when everybody was sweating in their pads and butting heads—everybody except the quarterback, who was wearing a sweat suit and flicking passes in a leisurely drill behind the goalposts.

chapter 13

By Thursday, Pearce was ready to write off the week as one of the worst—if not the very worst—he had ever dragged a football team through.

As the team jogged toward the dressing room after practice, Pearce realized with a jolt that he was genuinely worried now about Brenway College, even though Brenway had lost its first two games and showed no signs of getting better. The Marlin State drills had been flat and the players almost sullen as they went through the motions of practicing. From the week's first session on Monday afternoon, just after the appearance with Larry, Bruno, and Winnie at the alumni luncheon, Pearce had been devoting most of his time to keeping the lid on the bubbling resentment against Larry.

The first overt evidence of the extent of the problem cropped up even before the Monday practice session.

Pearce, walking through the dressing room in the early afternoon, a few minutes before the first of the players would be arriving to change into their practice suits, saw it and stopped in his tracks. There, pasted on Larry Hudson's locker, was a phosphorescent bumper sticker reading *Safety First.*

Pearce looked around. Nobody was in the dressing room except Jerry Phillips, the student manager, who was in a corner sorting some jerseys. Pearce glared at him and could see that Jerry, although keeping his head down and devoting unusual attention to his task, was watching the coach out of the corner of his eye.

"Jerry," Pearce barked.

The student manager looked around. "I don't know anything about it, Coach. Honest."

Pearce looked at him for a moment, then strode

over to the locker, peeled the sticker off, and tossed it in a wastebasket. "I'm glad you don't know anything about it, Jerry," he said. "And furthermore, you're not going to know anything about it. Do you understand?"

"Yes, sir."

Pearce knew that Jerry had been in the dressing room since the noon hour, preparing equipment for the week's practice, and probably had seen the person sticking the sign on Larry's locker. "I mean that this incident is not to be mentioned or discussed."

"Yes, sir."

Pearce had walked to his office with the uneasy feeling that the tone had been set for the week's practice, and the events of the coming days served only to reinforce the belief.

In the backfield drills, Winnie complained repeatedly about the way Larry was handing off the ball and making pitchouts. Joe Talmadge was openly loafing in practice—the worst of all signs. Louie Stetson retained his stone-faced composure, saying little. But it was disheartening to see him pass up the usual compliments, such as, "Nice pass," and instead walk by Larry without speaking.

The effect of it all on Larry seemed to be absolutely zero. He went about his assignments in a steady, workmanlike manner, neither smiling nor frowning, ignoring Winnie's remarks and clearly not seeking the compliments Louie Stetson was withholding. Pearce concluded that Larry had figured out for himself what would be coming from his teammates and had taken it into consideration when he decided to stick with the team. Larry's handling of the situation raised him even higher in the coach's estimation. It was part of what made a great quarterback—self-control and discipline, those two key ingredients in effective leadership.

Pearce had used those words—*self-control*, *discipline*, and *leadership*—when he telephoned Brad Hudson on Monday evening with the word of Larry's decision not to quit. But Pearce did not mention the bumper sticker reading *Safety First* and said nothing about the growing signs of trouble with the other players.

"That's great news, Coach," Brad Hudson had said, when Pearce told him of Larry's decision. "I'm sure he'll make it from here on out."

"We've got a long way to go," Pearce said. "But at least the first step has been taken."

Now as the practice week was drawing to a close, Pearce had good reason to wonder if the team itself would survive. A quarterback's self-control and discipline were valuable assets but how valuable in the face of a team rapidly becoming unable to function?

Bill Oliver was a regular observer during practice, and the veteran sports editor knew trouble when he saw it. "Well, Chuck, are you going to dump your flashy quarterback or throw out the best flanker back in the SIAA?" he asked, when he dropped into Pearce's office after practice.

Pearce got up and closed the door. "I hope you don't think you have to write anything about this," Pearce said.

Oliver shrugged. "Depends on what happens on Saturday. If they fall apart in front of Brenway College, I'll have to explain what happened."

"I don't think they'll fall apart."

"Maybe you don't need to play Larry at all," Oliver suggested. "You beat Central Teachers without him. Brenway is no better. Harry Willis could handle it."

Pearce had toyed with the idea. Oliver was right, of course. But what about the players? Would Winnie and Joe Talmadge and some of the others think they had bulldozed the coach into benching Larry? And what about the Marlin State fans who were coming out to see the new miracle quarterback and would be shouting for him the first time Harry Willis tossed a floater that got intercepted? And what about Larry Hudson? No, Pearce had decided, he had to play Larry, no matter what.

"Sure," Pearce said. "Harry could handle it. No doubt about it. And no doubt Harry will play a lot."

"I've heard that some of the linemen are saying they won't block for Larry."

"I do hope that doesn't happen," Pearce said, closing the conversation.

chapter 14

The weather for the Brenway College game, being played at home, matched Chuck Pearce's mood. Heavy rains had moved in during Friday night and continued through the noon hour on Saturday, right up to the kickoff time. Even though the rain stopped just at kickoff, heavy clouds hung darkly in the sky and threatened to resume their downpour at any minute and make the mushy field even worse.

Pearce looked it over glumly while the players went through their pregame warm-ups. He knew that this was no field for the fancy footwork of Winnie the Pooh. And even the running of Louie Stetson, although he did not have as shifty a style as Winnie, would be hampered in the muck of the field. The answer to the problem of a soggy field was simple: pass. And that meant Larry Hudson.

In a way, the weather helped Pearce get off the hook a little with the team. "That field out there is a mess," he told the players in the final moments before they took the field for the kickoff. "All of you know who benefits most from a muddy field—the lesser team. That means we've got our work cut out for us. This is a perfect day for the underdog to pull an upset. A good runner can't perform at his best. A wet ball is easy to fumble. If you get careless and give these guys a couple of breaks, you're going to find it mighty tough to come back. Brenway is hungry, and they think we're overconfident."

Pearce looked around the room. All of the players' eyes were on him. He hadn't said anything yet about the starting lineup, but he knew that none of them doubted who would be the choice at quarterback. They were just waiting for him to say it.

"The way to beat a wet field is to pass," Pearce went on. "So we're going to go with Larry throwing from the very start and hope to build up a quick lead, then hang on and take what we can get the rest of the way."

The Tigers trooped out of the dressing room and onto the field, and a light drizzle started.

Brenway College won the toss, and the fact did not go unnoticed by Pearce.

Brenway couldn't move after taking the opening kickoff and punted to Winnie the Pooh at the fifty. Winnie promptly slid and fell trying a sharp cut.

Larry shed his parka and jogged onto the field. On the first play he took the snap from center, faked to Louie Stetson off right tackle, and curled back to his right, cocking his arm and looking for Winnie downfield. He spotted him, far short of where the speedster would have been on a dry field, and uncorked the ball. Winnie and the ball came together on the ten-yard line, and Winnie churned over for the touchdown.

On the sideline, Pearce sighed with relief. He had called for the long bomb himself. There is nothing like a touchdown to make a team forget its internal problems, if only for a few minutes.

Again, Brenway College couldn't do anything on the kickoff and had to punt on fourth down from deep in its own territory.

Starting on the Brenway forty-five-yard line, Larry

alternated hand-offs to Louie and Burlington T. Johnson, and then rifled a short sideline pass to Eddie Evans for a first down on the Brenway thirty-four-yard line.

Pearce, watching closely, found himself breathing easier. Larry seemed to be moving smoothly into the rhythm of the game, with the shame of last Saturday and the snubs of the practice week behind him and forgotten. For now, at least, he was in business as a quarterback.

On the next play, a crossing pattern with Winnie and Eddie Evans out in front and fifteen yards downfield, Larry backpedaled quickly into the throwing position and set his feet for the pass. In the line, Joe Talmadge was struggling with a charging defensive lineman. Suddenly Joe lunged to his left, and a Brenway linebacker shot through the hole to Joe's right and began bearing down on Larry.

Larry turned and raced to his left to avoid the tackler. He was running in the wrong direction for a righthanded passer. But with Winnie breaking free in the secondary, and waving his right hand in the air for attention, Larry leaped, twisted his body to get his arm back at the right angle, and fired the pass.

Winnie got it and was nailed in his tracks. Larry fell in a heap from the momentum of his twisting leap.

Chuck Pearce had seen Joe Talmadge's lunge to the left. Joe had made the move a split second too early to see the charging linebacker coming over his right side. In any other game, Pearce would have written it off as a mistake, one of the rare mistakes in the notable college football career of Joe Talmadge. He would have made a mental note to chide Talmadge about it on Monday when the films were discussed. And then he would have dismissed it from his mind. But Pearce took the headphone from Cody and called Avery in the press box.

"What happened to Talmadge on that play?" he snapped. "That linebacker nearly got in there to break Larry in two."

"I don't know," Avery said. "Joe went to the left when he should've gone to the right, I guess. That's all."

Pearce handed the headphone back to Cody.

Larry's pass, while he had been leaping and twisting his body to throw from the wrong angle, had earned Marlin State a first down on the seventeen-yard line.

A pitchout to Winnie got eight yards and a handoff to Burlington T. Johnson picked up three through the middle for a first down on the six-yard line.

The drizzling rain continued to fall, and the Brenway College half of the field, where Marlin State had kept the game so far, was a slippery, soggy mess. Larry called a pass over the center to Winnie and put the ball right in his hands, but Winnie let it slip through.

From the sideline, Pearce squinted through the drizzling rain at Winnie, trotting back to the huddle. Anybody can drop a wet ball, Pearce told himself. But he couldn't help wondering about Winnie's error, just as he had wondered about Joe Talmadge's mistaken lunge to the left.

A moment later it didn't matter. Larry flipped a pass to Louie Stetson on the sideline, and the big fullback fell into the end zone for a touchdown.

With the score 14-0 and the first quarter barely two thirds gone, Pearce told Harry Willis to get himself ready to take over the next series.

chapter 15

The muddy, weary players enjoyed their showers quietly. They didn't behave as though they had walloped Brenway College 36-0. The only whooping and hollering came from Harry Willis. He always was the dressing-room cheerleader, making up for his lack of ability with enthusiasm. And this time he had a better reason than usual. He had played the rest of the game after the second touchdown, had passed for one touchdown, and had scored one himself.

Pearce watched Harry slapping people on the shoulder and shouting, "Attaway, attaway," and then he motioned Cody and Avery to his office.

"Well?" Pearce asked, when they were seated.

"You mean Talmadge," Avery said.

"And Winnie," Pearce said. "But let's talk about Talmadge first."

Cody leaned forward. "You're seeing ghosts, Chuck. Talmadge has made worse mistakes than that. He's a first-rate offensive tackle, but let's face it, anybody can make a mistake. If that linebacker had happened to take the other side, Talmadge would have had him dead in his tracks, and we'd be patting him on the back for it."

"You were upstairs, Avery. How did it look?"

"Like I told you on the phone. It just looked like he made a mistake. I agree with Cody. I think you're seeing ghosts. We all know about the bad feeling. Talmadge is part of it, and so is Winnie, but I don't think either of them would intentionally let the team down. The ball that Winnie dropped was wet, you know."

Pearce shrugged. "Okay. Maybe you're right. I hope so."

"Anyway," Cody said with a smile, "we won and we won big, and we're over the hump of playing a game after that business of Larry going down on his knee."

Pearce shook his head. "No, we're not over the hump. We're not over the hump at all. We've just bought a week. The matter's not dead and buried. It's just out of sight for the moment."

Pearce sat in the office long after Cody and Avery had left and Bill Oliver had come and gone and doodled lazy swirls on a pad of yellow paper. He was tearing the sheet of paper off the pad and wadding it up when a light knock came at the door.

"Come in."

Winnie stuck his head through the door. "Coach?"

"Come in, Winnie."

"We beat the socks off them," Winnie said. He smiled tentatively.

"Yes, we did. But there are tougher teams down the road. We have a long way to go."

"I know," Winnie said. He paused. "But that's not what I wanted to talk to you about, Coach."

"What's on your mind, Winnie?" Pearce suddenly felt very tired, and he hoped Winnie hadn't chosen this moment to make a pitch for Harry Willis at quarterback, based on the twenty-two points the Tigers had put on the board today under Harry's leadership.

"I don't know how to say this, but I want to say it, so I'll just go ahead," Winnie said, speaking slowly. "I didn't drop that ball in the end zone on purpose."

Pearce glared at him for a full minute. "Why did you feel you had to say that to me?"

Winnie bit his lower lip. "Because I thought about dropping the pass. I had shot my mouth off all week about Larry Hudson. You know, about his putting his knee down to keep from getting hit last week. And I knew that one way to put him back where he belongs would be to drop his passes."

"I see. But you didn't do it, did you?"

"I swear I didn't."

Pearce looked at Winnie, a smallish lad for a college football player, who had parlayed blinding speed and good hands and, above all, dedication and determination into all-conference honors. "Winnie, you'll make up for that dropped pass," Pearce said. "And I've already forgotten it."

Winnie left, and Pearce walked out behind him, got into his car, and drove home through the drizzling rain.

Maggie met him in the kitchen when he came from the garage. "You have a visitor," she said.

Pearce walked into the living room and found Joe Talmadge sitting on the couch. Joe stood up.

"Can I speak to you for a minute, Coach?"

"Sure, Joe. Sit down. What's on your mind?"

"I just want to tell you that I didn't let that linebacker in on Larry Hudson on purpose," he said, speaking with a fierce intensity. "I felt like a fool when it happened. I just committed myself too early, and he took advantage of it. I felt like a fool." He paused. "Everybody knows that I'd like to see Larry Hudson get smeared, after what he did last week against Warren Tech. But I didn't do it on purpose out there today, and I never would."

"Joe, you've made mistakes in the line before. Any lineman makes mistakes in the course of a game."

"Well, yeah, I guess so."

"This is the first time you ever felt you had to come around to me after the game and tell me that you didn't do it on purpose."

"Well. . . ."

"Well, what?"

"You know how everybody feels about that guy getting all the special treatment and then nearly losing the Warren Tech game for us just because he's afraid he might get bruised a little, and then he still comes out of the whole thing the big hero. You know what I mean."

"A good football team is composed of good people doing what they can do best, Joe, and that means tackles blocking in the line and quarterbacks passing, among other things," Pearce said.

Talmadge looked at him and nodded slightly.

Pearce leaned back. "Joe, when I was playing for Marlin State, we had a tackle who complained that the running backs got all the glory while the tackles just got bloody. And one day, when we were pasting this very same Brenway College team by something like forty points in the fourth quarter, Coach Brightman put this tackle in at fullback with orders to the quarterback to give him the ball."

Pearce paused a moment. "You know what happened? The tackle tried to run the ball. He didn't do badly. He made about five yards. But he got hit at least six times and hit hard, and he came off the field swearing he would never carry the ball again, because everybody on the field was trying to knock him down. That tackle stopped complaining about the ball carriers having such a good deal."

Joe grinned. "I see what you mean."

"And, Joe," Pearce said. "One other thing: I was that tackle."

chapter 16

The buildup for the Oakman State game got under way immediately and was so intense that neither Chuck Pearce nor his players had much time to worry about why Larry Hudson wouldn't run with the ball or what the effect might be on the team.

While Marlin State had been whipping a mediocre Brenway College team 36-0 in the mud, the Oakman

State Hornets had massacred tough Warren Tech by a 31-0 score. The victory was the third in a row for Oakman State, giving the Hornets a record identical to the Marlin State mark, setting the stage for the battle of the unbeatens.

But there was more to it than that, Pearce thought, as he read the Sunday-morning papers in his office after watching the Brenway College films.

Oakman State had been underrated in the preseason guessing about who had a powerhouse, much as Marlin State had been sold short. Warren Tech had been the favorite to win the championship a second year in a row until Marlin State unveiled its mystery quarterback and scored an upset. That put Marlin State at the top of the heap. But at the same time, Oakman State was winning its first two games and now had whipped Warren Tech worse than Marlin State had. Pearce wasn't one to put much stock in comparative scores, but the fact was there, nevertheless.

Another point that hit Pearce square between the eyes was Oakman State's defensive record. The Hornets had not been scored on in their first three games. Pearce knew that beyond the obvious fact that they had a good defense, the unscored-on record would serve as a tremendous morale factor in the coming game. The Oakman State defense would be determined to keep its slate clean. Pride counted for a lot on a football field, Pearce knew, and the Oakman State defenders would be fighting ferociously to keep Marlin State from crossing the goal line even once.

Traditionally, Marlin State and Oakman State met on neutral ground, in Memorial Stadium in Capitol City. The custom had its roots twenty years back when campus raids by enthusiastic students before the games, and fights after the games, almost forced the schools to terminate the series. They settled on the compromise arrangement of a neutral site and never had given it up. The large stadium in Capitol City always assured both schools of their largest crowd of the season. And this year, with both teams undefeated, both of them victors over the highly touted Warren Tech, and Oakman State still unscored on, all the ingredients were there for a titanic struggle and a record crowd.

The newspapers billed the battle between Marlin State and Oakman State as the "championship" game of the SIAA, with the winner deemed certain to ride roughshod over the rest of the teams on the schedule and probably get a bid from one of the small-college bowl games. The sportswriters lost no time in picking their favorite: Oakman State. Even Bill Oliver pointed out that Oakman State's defense was every bit as good as the record indicated. And he noted, to Pearce's dismay, that "Marlin State has reportedly been having some morale problems, and they are related to the miracle quarterback that the Tigers sprung on Warren Tech with such devastating results, Larry Hudson." Oliver knew more than he was saying, Pearce was sure, but he wished the hometown sports editor had not felt he needed to mention the problem at all.

Pearce was dropping the paper into a wastebasket when Maggie came in with sandwiches. "Where are Cody and Avery?" she asked.

"They've gone to pick up Rudy," he said, reaching for a sandwich as Maggie turned to leave. "These look good. Thanks a lot."

Rudy Bostick was an insurance salesman who had played for Marlin State ten years ago, at the same time Avery had played, and he handled some scouting assignments on a volunteer basis. Nobody in the SIAA had sufficient coaching staff to scout all the opponents, but everybody had volunteers such as Rudy who would attend important games and report back with their notebooks full of diagrams and scribbled impressions of weaknesses and strengths. Rudy's assignment had been Oakman State's game with Warren Tech.

"Here we are," Rudy said, leading Cody and Avery into Pearce's office, "but you're not going to like what I've got to say."

"From the papers," Pearce said, "it looks like we shouldn't even bother to show up."

Rudy laughed. "They're tough, that's true. But I've got some things here that will interest you."

The four of them sat around Pearce's desk, and Rudy opened a blue, loose-leaf binder and began speaking in a low monotone as he slowly turned the pages.

On Wednesday, before driving to Capitol City with Bill Oliver for a televised news conference with the Oakman State coach, Pearce did something he never had done before in his six years at the helm of the Marlin State football team. He closed the practice session. Campus police swept the area of all onlookers—students, trusted fans, sportswriters, and some strangers who undoubtedly were observing for Oakman State's coaching staff. There was some grumbling, and the loudest came from Henry Osgood, the president of the alumni association.

"Pearce," he announced in a loud voice, "this is an insult."

"Believe me, Henry, it's necessary," Pearce replied, and tried to walk away.

Osgood followed Pearce out onto the field. "The very idea that I can't be trusted . . . ."

"Henry," Pearce said patiently, "if anybody stays, I've got to let everybody stay. Don't you see? I can't bar the students and let the alumni stay."

"It's this trouble about Hudson, isn't it?" Osgood suddenly blurted.

"No, Henry, it isn't."

"We've all heard about the trouble," Osgood persisted.

"Don't believe everything you hear, Henry."

"If you don't handle this thing, Pearce, well, you know. . . ."

"That's exactly what I'm doing, Henry—handling it. Now will you please go so we can clear the area and get to work."

Osgood left in a storm, and Pearce called the players around him in a group as the last of the spectators were shooed out of the area.

Later, in Bill Oliver's car on the way to Capitol City, Oliver held his silence as long as he could. "A closed practice usually means a team is working on some surprises for Saturday's game," Oliver said.

"That's sort of it," Pearce said.

"Sort of?"

Pearce paused, then said, "Bill, the secret is really

no secret at all. It's just that Oakman State has not had much of a chance to see Larry Hudson. You know, he sat out the Central Teachers game, and then after playing against Warren Tech he sat out most of the Brenway game. They may have scouted our game with Warren Tech. I don't know. But either way they haven't got much of a book on Larry, and they want to know all they can find out. We've been having large numbers of strangers at practice, so I closed it today. That's all, honest."

Oliver drove along without saying anything.

"Oh, sure," Pearce added with a smile after a moment, "we're adding some new wrinkles. Everybody does that, and you know it."

"Chuck, I thought maybe it had something to do with what Henry Osgood was bellowing about," Oliver said.

"You know Henry."

"But," Oliver asked, "is the trouble as bad as I hear? After all, I saw Joe Talmadge go the wrong way and let that linebacker through last week."

"Bill, anybody can make a mistake, and that includes Joe Talmadge."

"I also saw you take the headphone and call upstairs," Bill said. "You were asking Avery about what he saw from up there in the press box."

Pearce cast a hard glance at the bespectacled sports editor, but Oliver kept his face to the front as he drove. "Did Avery tell you that?"

Oliver smiled. "No, but you just did."

"Let's change the subject," Pearce said.

The press conference in the television station's studio was a regular prelude to the annual Capitol City game between Marlin State and Oakman State. In other years the two coaches had answered the questions of the station's sportscaster and a couple of newspaper reporters, and probably not very many people bothered to tune in. There had been too many years recently when either Marlin State or Oakman State, or both, had a poor record and none of the fans in the neutral site were excited about the game. But this year was different, and Pearce found himself facing half a dozen reporters.

Pearce always felt uneasy on television, and the feeling was even worse now. He didn't want to be asked on television about the reports of dissension on his team. A denial in such a case always sounded hollow and left everybody asking, "Well, what else could he say?"

While Pearce squirmed uncomfortably, the Oakman State coach, Jimmy Arnold, was the absolute picture of confidence, fielding questions with quips for answers and obviously enjoying himself immensely.

"Do you think your Hornets can maintain their unscored-on record against Marlin State?"

"The boys tell me that the only thing they fear is a running quarterback," Arnold snapped back with a smile, sure that his meaning was getting through.

Pearce squirmed some more. The word was out, no doubt. Oakman State had good reason to suspect that Larry Hudson would not run with the ball. For anyone who doubted it after Larry's display against Warren Tech, the Brenway College game offered some pretty convincing evidence.

"We figure," Arnold said, "that we can stop any passer who is trying to throw with one knee on the ground."

Some of the reporters exchanged brief glances, obviously feeling that Arnold was going too far, possibly with the idea of inflaming the feelings of the Marlin State players—including Larry Hudson—who might be watching. Pearce could imagine how Joe Talmadge felt about blocking for a quarterback who was letting the team in for such ridicule. And he knew that Winnie the Pooh would flush and cringe.

The one good result of Arnold's needling remarks was that the reporters, when the time came to question Pearce, felt he already had been dragged over the coals enough about Larry Hudson and team dissension, and they didn't refer to the matter at all. The closest they came to opening the gate to the subject was the question, "Coach Pearce, can your offense score on the Oakman State defense?"

"Let me answer you this way: you have to score to win, and we expect to win."

"You closed your practice session to the public this afternoon. Does that mean you have some surprises in store for Oakman State?"

"Of course it does." Pearce smiled. "Or at least we hope they will be surprises. But I'm not going to tell you what they are."

The press conference ended without any more cracks out of Jimmy Arnold.

Pearce mentioned the Oakman State coach's performance to Bill Oliver in the car on the trip back to Marlin State.

"He was just trying to psych you," Oliver said. "You and the players. I don't think it was very smart."

"Why do you say that?"

"Sometimes that sort of thing can have the opposite of the desired effect."

Pearce considered Oliver's analysis and decided that he was wrong this time. It wasn't hard to visualize the effect on Larry Hudson, who had to function effectively as a leader if Marlin State was to have a chance of victory. And Pearce could imagine the effect on the other players, already resentful of Larry's going to one knee when they needed the yardage against Warren Tech to win. The fact that Larry had led the team to the winning touchdown hardly mattered. Nobody had forgotten the chilling feeling when Larry's dominant instinct had made him willing to take a ten-yard loss rather than risk a moment of pain.

"No," Pearce said, "I think Jimmy Arnold had it sized up about right."

chapter 17

When Chuck Pearce walked onto the field and looked back up into the grandstands, the ushers were setting up folding chairs in the aisles and along the front of the stands to accommodate the overflow crowd. The sun was bright and the air had the crispness of autumn—the classic weather for a college football game.

Pearce walked toward his team going through calisthenics at one end of the field and looked back at the other end of the field for a glimpse of the Oakman State squad. Jimmy Arnold was standing in front of them, his hands thrust into the pockets of his green-and-gold Oakman State parka.

The stands filled as the minutes passed, and it was time for Pearce to hail the Tigers back into the dressing room for one last moment before the kickoff.

Pearce climbed onto a bench and looked around the dressing room, pausing a few seconds until he had the attention of everyone in the room. The practice week had been a strange one, coldly businesslike, with no horsing around and no flares of temper, almost totally unemotional. That could be good, meaning that every last man understood the task that faced him and was determined to be ready. Or it could be bad, meaning that a flat, emotionless game would come out of what had, in fact, been a dull practice week. Pearce wished he knew which was the case. Well, he thought, I'll know in just a few minutes, because the tenor of the game is bound to show up early.

"I'm not much for pep talks," Pearce began. "When I was a player, I thought they were corny. I still do. But before we go out there I want to tell you that you're good men playing a game that you know well. That means that you can win—if you have the will to win. I believe that, or I wouldn't be here today. And you believe it, or you would not be here.

"I'll level with you and tell you that this is the most important college game I have ever coached," Pearce said and paused, wondering how many of the players understood the full implications of the statement. His job was on the line this year, whether they knew it or not, or whether they cared. "And this is the most important college game you'll ever play. You will look back on this one forty years from now, and you'll remember everything about it. Now go out there and make damned sure that you can be proud of your memories."

Pearce jumped off the bench and led the Tigers on the run out the door and down the ramp to the field.

Marlin State won the toss, and Pearce smiled at that good omen. Today every little thing counted. Bruno Chinigo told the officials that Marlin State chose to receive the kickoff. Oakman State had the choice of goals, but it didn't matter on a day such as this, clear and still and windless.

The players gathered around Pearce on the sideline and jumped and slapped each other on the shoulders in the final ritual of enthusiasm before taking the field. Burlington T. Johnson started shouting, "Score, score, score," and the others picked it up. The roar from the knot of players on the sidelines swept across the field to Oakman State's bench and up the grandstand to the fans.

The eleven men of the kickoff-return team took the field, with Johnson and Winnie the Pooh deep, as Oakman State lined up for the kickoff. Johnson jogged in place slowly as he waited. Winnie touched his toes several times.

The twenty-four other Marlin State players lined the sideline. One of them, Larry Hudson, stood off by himself, to the right, almost down to the thirty-yard line at the end of the field where Johnson and Winnie were waiting for the kickoff.

The kickoff was a low rifle shot, straight at Johnson. It was the kind of kick a runner loves. Johnson gathered in the ball and raced straight forward, veering toward the sidelines, where the line of Marlin State blockers was setting up a corridor. Because of the low kick, the Oakman State defenders didn't have the time they needed to get down the field and nail him, and Johnson rambled from the twelve-yard line to the thirty-yard line before he hit a traffic jam of defenders trying to break through the wall of blockers. Joe Talmadge leveled three tacklers with a flying block. He was horizontal and waist high when he hit them, and all four went down in a tangle of arms and legs, while Johnson spurted past the pile to the forty-yard line. A tackler laid a hand on him at the forty-five-yard line, but Johnson spun away and kept his feet. The movement took him outside his wall of blockers, however, and he found himself racing back toward midfield, virtually unprotected and on his own. He was going against the grain of the defense, though, and the tacklers overshot him as he crossed the fifty-yard line and wriggled his way into Oakman State territory. Ducking and squirming, he was hit from behind and downed at the Oakman State forty-two-yard line.

When Johnson finally was brought down, Larry shed his parka and jogged onto the field along with Max Ford, going into the game to give Johnson a chance to catch his breath. Johnson was smiling as he came off the field.

Pearce squinted through the bright sunlight as the offense huddled around Larry at the fifty-yard line.

Oakman State's poor kickoff had given Marlin State a big break at the outset of the game, and the Tigers had taken advantage of it, springing Johnson forty-six yards down the field and into Oakman State territory. But now came the test of whether Marlin State could turn the good break into a touchdown.

In the Marlin State grandstands, the fans had taken up the chant, "Score, score, score." They knew, as well as Pearce and the players, that any kind of a score against Oakman State's proud defense would give the Tigers a tremendous boost this early in the game.

Pearce eyed the Oakman State defense. They had one linebacker fewer than usual. In his place, they had another defensive halfback. Pearce wasn't surprised. They were gambling that their superior defense could hold the Marlin State ground game with less than the usual muscle up front and that the extra speedster in the secondary would stifle Larry Hudson's aerial game.

Pearce shouted at Larry and pointed to the defense. Larry nodded.

Larry handed off to Louie Stetson over right tackle on the first play, and Louie banged his way for four yards. Pearce unconsciously nodded and agreed with the wisdom of the call, a safe and conservative beginning for the series, always a smart move when the opponent is as tough as Oakman State. This was no time for taking wild chances. Maybe later, but not now.

On the next play Larry shoveled the ball out to Max Ford, who was circling wide to the left. Ford got the pitchout and tried to cut back to the inside but was tackled on the spot for a loss of one yard. Pearce had started to send Johnson back into the backfield, but he held off now. One of his long-standing rules was never to take a runner out of the game right after a loss of yardage.

Now it was third down and seven yards to go, and nobody on either side doubted the play that was coming up—a Larry Hudson pass, probably to Winnie the Pooh but maybe to Eddie Evans.

Larry called the play, and Marlin State lined up. Winnie was out in a wide flanker position. In front of him, Eddie Evans lined up at split end. Eddie would go deep, and Winnie would circle to the sideline in a shorter pattern. The primary receiver was Winnie.

Larry took the snap and backpedaled quickly into the pocket, not bothering with the fake hand-off that would have fooled nobody in this situation.

Eddie was racing downfield with an Oakman State defender matching him stride for stride. And off to the sideline, Winnie faked inside and turned to the outside only to run into a logjam of Oakman State defenders. Somehow the Oakman State defense had managed to have three men in Winnie's territory with another defender tracking Eddie far down the field without leaving anybody open for the pass.

Time was running out for Larry in the pocket when

Winnie cut and dashed back to the inside and looked open for a second. In that second, Larry fired the ball. The pass was a good one, a rifle shot straight on the mark, but the crowd of Oakman State defenders had recovered from Winnie's faking movements, and one of the halfbacks got there at the same moment that Winnie and the ball came together. They fought for a fraction of a second, and the Oakman State defender won. Winnie brought down the interceptor on the twenty-nine-yard line.

Larry turned and walked from the field. Chinigo, coming on, clapped him on the shoulder pads and said, "Tough luck." Larry didn't reply.

When Larry reached the sideline, Pearce was on the headphone with Avery and Rudy in the press box above, and he gestured to Larry to join him. "Right, right, right," Pearce was barking into the phone, as Larry walked up to him.

Pearce turned to Larry. "They've got an extra halfback in there to stop the passes. It's enough of a secondary to combine a zone defense with man-to-man coverage of Winnie."

"It was a crowd," Larry said.

"Winnie got himself caught in the seam of the zone, with those two defenders, and he also had to contend with the special man assigned to him,"

Pearce said. "It amounted to triple coverage of Winnie."

"Eddie wasn't free either," Larry said. "You'd think that Eddie going so deep would pull some of that defense off of Winnie."

"They've got confidence in their individuals," Pearce said. "One man on Eddie going deep is enough, if that man is good enough, and they're sure that he is."

Larry nodded.

"We've got two choices," Pearce said. "One is to send Louie and Burlington pounding in there so much that they have to give up that extra pass defender and put the linebacker in there. And the other is to use Winnie as a decoy and dump the passes off to Louie and Burlington—short, quick passes into the flat."

"Sure," Larry said.

Pearce knew there was a third alternative—keeper runs around end by the quarterback. Nothing cracked a tight pass defense like a quarterback loping along the line of scrimmage with the option of passing or running. If the defense hung back for a pass, the quarterback chewed up the yards on the ground. But Pearce did not mention it. Neither did Larry.

Pearce glared hard at Larry. "Got it?"

chapter 18

Oakman State tried three running plays and, on fourth down and three to go, sent a high punt spiraling to Winnie, who called for a fair catch and downed it on the Marlin State twenty-five-yard line.

Louie Stetson's thundering plunges into the middle of the line, mixed with some fancy scampering around end by Winnie moved Marlin State to a first down on the thirty-seven-yard line. But the gains on the ground failed to frighten Oakman State into abandoning its plan of an extra halfback in place of a linebacker to stop Larry Hudson's passes.

The Oakman rushers were virtually ignoring Larry as soon as the play showed the first clear signs of being a run. Larry was simply the relay point for the ball going from the center to Louie or Winnie or Burlington for a run, and the Oakman State defenders knew it.

At the forty-two-yard line, with second down and five yards to go, Larry called a pass in the huddle. It was time to see if the series of runs had lulled the Oakman State defense into the assumption that Larry had given up throwing.

Taking the snap, Larry turned and faked a handoff to Louie slamming into the line. And, sure enough, the defensive halfbacks rushed forward to help back up the line. Larry, with the ball on his hip, let the momentum of his turning carry him out to the right.

By the time the Oakman State defense spotted what was happening, Larry was cocking his arm and firing the ball at Winnie, who was running deep. Winnie had a defender with him, but a half step behind. Larry led Winnie more than usual, and

Winnie reached out and tipped the ball, juggled it for a moment, and finally gathered it in on the run at the Oakman State forty-one-yard line. The defender lunged frantically, but Winnie's half-step advantage had been fatal. The long lead on the pass had enabled Winnie to take in the ball without slowing, and the defender crashed to the ground without touching Winnie just as Winnie cut to his right, raced downfield, and crossed the goal line.

The Marlin State stands erupted in a roar. On the Oakman State side, the fans settled back in their seats with a deadly quiet. Jimmy Arnold stood motionless, staring in disbelief.

Winnie barely got out of the end zone for his jog back to the bench before a crowd of Marlin State players surrounded him, shouting and pummeling him. At midfield, Louie Stetson got up from the crowd of tacklers he had attracted by plunging empty-handed into the line and rushed forward to join the melee. Larry turned and trotted off the field.

On the scoreboard, the lights blinked and settled down to read 6-0 and then, after the kick, blinked again and settled into a 7-0 reading.

Pearce clapped Larry on the shoulder pads when he came to the sideline, and he slapped Winnie the Pooh on the rump. It had been a daring call, a pass on second and five with the defense stacked against the pass. But the fake to Louie had been perfect, giving Winnie the half-step advantage he needed going downfield. And the pass had been the closest to absolutely perfect that Pearce had ever seen. It forced Winnie to increase his speed a notch and stretch for the ball, having the effect of pulling him away from the defender.

Pearce looked at the clock. The first quarter had almost ticked away.

On the field, Mitch Reynolds adjusted the ball on the kicking tee at the forty-yard line, and the Marlin State kickoff team aligned itself for the charge downfield. Mitch's kick sailed high and straight to the five-yard line, where Oakman State's deep man gathered it in and started back up the field, running straight up the middle.

Pearce, kneeling on the sideline and nibbling a blade of grass, had an uneasy feeling almost immediately. The Oakman State blockers converged at the thirty-yard line, and they had the split second they needed to get themselves set, forming a cocoon for the ball carrier to charge into. Pearce fretted. They shouldn't have had the split second they needed. The Marlin State defense should have been there busting up the pattern before the blockers had a chance to get set.

The ball carrier made it to the back side of the shell of blockers, raced through, and burst out the other side near the forty-yard line, with two of his blockers out in front of him.

Pearce involuntarily stood up.

A savage block delayed Bruno Chinigo for only a moment, but it was enough, and Chinigo went out of the play, left behind. The ball carrier crossed the fifty-yard line with clear sailing ahead. Marty White, the last man with a chance, got a hand on the ball carrier, but only lightly, before the last blocker cut him down.

Chinigo was giving chase at the finish, but it was a futile effort, and he was ten yards back when the runner crossed the goal.

Pearce turned and lowered his head.

The kick made it 7-7.

chapter 19

The parade of players into the Marlin State dressing room at the half time moved slowly. Bruno Chinigo was breathing heavily, the result of a second quarter that had seen the Marlin State defense on the field almost all the way, battling against the grinding running game of Oakman State. Louie Stetson, the bull of the Marlin State offense, was limping with a thigh bruise. Joe Talmadge had the badly scraped hands and arms that are the badge of a tackle.

Throughout the grueling second quarter, Oakman State had threatened time and again. But the Marlin State defense had risen up at the moment of need, clamped the gate shut, and kept the Hornets from scoring.

Still, the second quarter had belonged to Oakman State, no doubt about it. Marlin State had managed to cling to the 7-7 tie, but only the superior play of the defense at the critical moments had accomplished the task. Oakman State's offense had enough power to control the ball, even though it had been unable to push across another score. And Oakman's vaunted defense was measuring up to its advance billing. Except for the one slip in the first quarter, when Larry had fooled them on a hand-off to Louie Stetson and then zipped the perfect pass to Winnie, Oakman's defenders had succeeded in bottling up Marlin State's runners and covering the pass receivers.

Larry walked into the dressing room and sat on a bench facing the table where Chuck Pearce was looking at sheafs of yellow paper with Cody and Avery. Larry had completed three of seven passes, with one interception, in the first half. Except for the scoring pass to Winnie, his completions had amounted to a couple of short gainers. They were the kinds of completions the Oakman State defense would be willing to surrender in return for stopping the runs and holding off the full threat of Larry's throwing arm.

Pearce looked up and got the attention of the players, then nodded to Avery.

"A couple of things are obvious from upstairs," Avery said. "The first one you already know, but I'll tell you about it anyway. Oakman's zone defense with a rover back chasing Winnie is covering that secondary like a blanket. We don't dare throw into it, and they know it."

Avery paused a moment and looked at one of the yellow sheets of paper. "But they're sliding into an interesting pattern as the game goes on. When Larry backpedals into the pocket, they wait a second to check for a hand-off, and then they start dropping back fast, and it's been working. When Larry rolls out, they don't wait even that one second. They start falling back. They were pretty cautious in the first quarter, but they're becoming less so as the game goes on. Near the end of the half, they were beginning to start falling back the instant Larry made his turn.

"So it's clear that when Larry is backpedaling he's got another second to find a receiver open," Avery said. "And when he's rolling out . . . well, a pass is really out of the question, but a runner taking a pitchout may gain a stride with a draw play."

Avery nodded to Pearce, and Pearce said, "Cody's got some words for the defense. Look at the blackboard over there."

Cody led off with a diagram of how Oakman State had sprung its runner loose for a touchdown on the kickoff return. "We're kicking off to start the second half," Cody said slowly. "And we don't want to give them another touchdown."

From there he moved through a series of suggestions for linemen, linebackers, and the secondary to meet the offense wrinkles that Oakman State had used to surprise Marlin State in the first half.

"We've just a minute or two left," Pearce said, when Cody had finished, "and I'm going to tell you what the second half is going to be like."

The players looked up, a little surprised at his tone.

"The third quarter is going to be a rerun of the second quarter, tough and grinding, and we've got to hold them," Pearce said. "And we'll score in the fourth quarter and win."

Pearce paused and the players watched him closely. The matter-of-fact way that Pearce outlined the scenario was puzzling.

"Remember this," he said softly. "If we are within one touchdown of winning when we go into the fourth quarter, we'll win. It's up to you to make sure that we are either out front or within striking distance at the end of the third quarter. The third quarter is vital. Absolutely vital."

He nodded to Chinigo, who stood up and said, "Let's go," and led the team out of the dressing room.

Avery and Rudy already had left to return to the press box. Cody fell in beside Pearce behind the last of the players in the corridor leading from the dressing room to the field.

He looked at Pearce. "Do you know something I don't?"

Pearce smiled. "I don't know. I really don't know. But we're going to find out."

chapter 20

Chuck Pearce knelt on the sideline and watched Mitch Reynolds place the ball on the kicking tee. Mitch's kick soared high and straight, a carbon copy of the kick that Oakman State had run back for a touchdown in the first quarter.

This time the Oakman State middle receiver, taking in the ball on the seven-yard line, swung to his left and handed off to a back curling behind him. Pearce watched his onrushing defense react to the reverse in perfect form and chase the ball carrier out of bounds on the twenty-one-yard line.

From there, Oakman State launched into its bruising ground game, which had monopolized the second quarter, eating up the yardage in small bits and controlling the ball. If Jimmy Arnold had any surprises up his sleeve for the second half, he wasn't showing them yet. The pattern so far was the standard Oakman State fare of fullback plunges into the middle and halfback sweeps of the ends.

Bruno Chinigo called the signals on defense from his middle linebacker slot, shouted words of encouragement, and moved up and down the line, slapping the interior linemen on the rump. But his steps weren't as bouncy as usual, and he seemed weary as he slouched into the ready position each time just before the snap of the ball.

Oakman State marched to a first down on the fifty with a low-slung fullback, strong as a horse, carrying into the line on every other play.

Pearce glanced up at the clock from his kneeling position on the sideline. More than five minutes of the third quarter had passed.

On first down, the Oakman State quarterback

faded quickly into what was going to be a pass play. The move, especially on first down, caught the Marlin State defenders off-balance. This was only the third pass of the game for Oakman State, which hadn't shown much inclination to pass in any of its games so far. The quarterback had good protection and the time he needed to look for his receivers racing deep into Marlin State territory. He fired toward the sideline, where a receiver was racing past the thirty-yard line.

Randy Garrett, a sophomore safety, was with him. The ball was on target. Both players went into the air for it. The thud of their collision in midair could be heard across the field, where Pearce was now on his feet. The two players came down together in a heap, and the ball landed out of bounds.

Pearce looked anxiously at the official, fearing an interference call. He sighed when he saw the official turn his back on the play and walk back toward the line of scrimmage. Arnold was five yards onto the field screaming at the official that his receiver had been blocked while trying to make the catch, but the official ignored him.

Three plays later Oakman State punted. Winnie fielded the kick and ran back eight yards to the eighteen-yard line.

The plunges of Louie Stetson and the slants of Burlington T. Johnson, with an occasional pitchout to Winnie around the ends, got three first downs and placed Marlin State on Oakman's forty-seven-yard line with a little more than three minutes left in the third quarter.

Pearce looked from the clock to the blinking lights telling the score: 7-7. He watched Larry walking toward the huddle, and in the brief second that their eyes met Pearce understood the question in his quarterback's glance and he nodded slightly. Yes, try a pass, the first aerial of the second half for Marlin State.

Larry took the snap and backpedaled quickly. The flashing form of Winnie was racing parallel to the line of scrimmage, his right hand extended and waving in the air.

The ball zipped through the crowd of onrushing linemen toward the spot where Willie's running should carry him to a completion. But Winnie's lunge was not enough, and the pass flew by his outstretched fingers and into the arms of an Oakman State halfback rushing up for what he thought would be a tackle. The Oakman State halfback was as surprised as anyone with the interception and fell on the spot trying to make a quick cut.

It was Oakman State's ball on the Oakman State forty-five-yard line. Larry trudged off the field.

Winnie trotted past him and mumbled, "Sorry."

Larry turned. "My fault. Bad pass," he said.

Bruno Chinigo and his weary crew of defenders moved back onto the field to fight the savage blocks and bullish runs of the Oakman State offense.

Five rushing plays and a short pass carried Oakman State to the Marlin State thirty-nine-yard line as the last minute of the third quarter began to tick away. Oakman State lined up for the snap, the quarterback took the ball and began backpedaling, veering to his left.

"Pass," shouted Chinigo.

But then the quarterback, without breaking the stride of his backpedaling, flipped the ball gently to a halfback waiting at his right.

"Halfback pass," shouted Chinigo, swerving his charge to chase the new ball carrier.

The halfback retreated a couple of paces, peering downfield, and cocked his arm. Then, out of nowhere, a runner swept behind the halfback and took the ball out of his hand, tucked it in, and started racing toward the opposite sideline.

"Reverse, reverse," shouted Chinigo, but it was too late.

The runner had the field to himself by the time he crossed the line of scrimmage. Marlin State's defenders, having changed course twice already to keep up with the play, found themselves on the wrong side of the field and moving the wrong way, about as completely out of position as defensive players could possibly be.

The runner scored without a hand being laid on him.

Pearce had stood up when the quarterback first had begun to backpedal and was veering to his left. Something was funny, Pearce knew, and he wanted to shout a warning to his players. But he couldn't read the play himself at that point, and the variation on the old Statue of Liberty play caught him completely by surprise.

The last seconds of the third quarter were on the clock.

The fans in the Marlin State grandstand were shouting, "Block that kick," and a weary Bruno Chinigo was running up and down behind the line of scrimmage urging his teammates to do just that.

But Bruno himself was the one who did it. With the snap from center he launched himself in a leaping, shouting charge, arms stretched skyward, and broke through the Oakman State line. He felt the ball graze his left hand just as he went down in a tumble of bodies. He turned, on his knees, in time to see the official's sideways arm gesture, signaling no good. The scoreboard stood unchanged, 13-7. Bruno Chinigo was smiling as he got to his feet.

On the sideline, Cody appeared beside Pearce. "Well," he said, "they did it. We're within striking distance in the fourth quarter."

Pearce said, "Yes, they did it. Now we've got to win."

chapter 21

Oakman State sent the kickoff booming into the end zone. Burlington T. Johnson backed up and gathered in the ball. He surveyed the field and quickly downed the ball for a touchback.

Larry dropped his parka and jogged onto the field to begin the drive at the twenty-yard line.

From the sideline, Pearce stared at the back of

Larry's jersey as the quarterback moved out to call the team around him in the huddle.

Pearce had been directing his talk at Larry more than anyone else when, before the game, he had told the team that this was an afternoon they would remember for the rest of their lives. And he had been sending a message to Larry when he told the team at the half time that the third quarter was absolutely vital. Now, as he looked at thc crouching figure of Larry Hudson leaning into the huddle, Pearce felt that this very series of downs, starting at the twenty-yard line in the opening seconds of the fourth quarter, would make all the difference. For the two teams on the field, the next few minutes would decide the game's winner. For the Marlin State Tigers, the coming plays would decide the entire season. And for Larry Hudson, the moment at hand would mark a turning point in his life.

Pearce watched as the Tigers moved out of the huddle and lined up. His face showed nothing as he knelt on the sideline and stared blankly at the scene on the field. He thought it strange, and in a way wonderful, that a game, a football season, and a life had these few special moments that meant success or failure, without regard for what had gone before. As he watched the players lining up, he had the inescapable feeling that one of those special moments was upon him. It was coming—now, any second now.

Two off-tackle smashes by Louie Stetson and an end sweep by Johnson got Marlin State a first down on the thirty-one-yard line. The Tigers were moving, but they couldn't make the whole eighty-yard drive on the ground, and it would be tough completing a pass against an Oakman State defense stacked for the pass.

With the first down, Larry was standing outside the huddle, waiting for the players to settle into place. He turned and glanced at the sideline, catching Pearce's eye. Pearce thought he detected a barely perceptible nod, and he found himself unconsciously nodding in return.

Pearce knelt, plucked his blade of grass, and stuck it into his mouth. He felt that he had received the message as clearly as if Larry had spoken to him. It was the glance he had been waiting for.

As Larry ducked into the huddle, Pearce felt that he knew the words his quarterback was saying: "Quarterback option, oh-eight-oh." Those were the words that meant Larry would roll out and run to his right, with Winnie trailing for a pitchout. It was a quarterback running play, designed for Winnie to be a decoy, enabling the quarterback to duck back inside and run. The situation fairly screamed for the play, especially in the light of Oakman State's undisguised certainty that Larry would not run with the ball.

When the Tigers broke out of the huddle and headed for the line, Joe Talmadge was smiling. And Winnie, the great disbeliever, was wearing a puzzled expression. Pearce said the words, softly but aloud: "Quarterback option, oh eight oh." Nothing else would make Joe Talmadge come out of the huddle smiling like that. And nothing less would have put that stunned expression on Winnie's face.

Larry took the snap and began to roll out to his right immediately. Winnie was swinging out behind him, racing for the sideline. The Oakman State defense reacted instantly. The defensive backs faded into their zone defense without hesitation, concentrating on the flying form of Eddie Evans. The linemen zeroed in on Winnie, who was going wide.

Larry was behind his end now. Louie Stetson was bursting through the line for blocking help downfield. Winnie was moving into his cut, a little behind Larry and six yards outside him. Joe Talmadge was letting a tackler get away from him intentionally to chase Winnie. That would get one tackler out of the way for sure.

Cocking his head first toward Eddie Evans, deep downfield veering to the sideline, and then turning for a fake to Winnie, Larry cut back inside and charged straight for the broad back of Joe Talmadge. The hole was there. Talmadge had let the one tackler escape him, and that man was beyond Larry now and running the wrong way before he realized what was happening. And Joe leveled a linebacker just as Larry crossed the line of scrimmage.

All the fans on both sides were on their feet. They knew that Larry Hudson simply did not run with the football. But there he was, picking his way through a hole blasted in the line by Joe Talmadge. In the press box, even Bill Oliver, who never got excited about anything after his years of watching football games for a living, was on his feet, and he was smiling.

On the Marlin State sideline, Chuck Pearce stood with his hands on his hips and stared intently at the play unfolding in front of him. Behind Pearce, the players on the bench leaped to their feet and let out a cheer as Larry tucked the ball away and cut back into the hole in the line. At the Oakman State sideline, Jimmy Arnold was shouting something to his players on the field, but nobody could hear him above the din.

By the time Larry was stepping across the line of

scrimmage, the Oakman State linemen were wildly trying to reverse their course. But they were too late. The defensive backs were either out of the play, chasing Eddie Evans far downfield, or they were roaming far enough back in their zone pass defense to be sitting ducks for the Marlin State blockers.

Louie Stetson's hurtling form cleared a path for Larry near midfield, and Larry danced around the tangle of arms and legs and raced into Oakman State territory. Oakman State's defense proved that it deserved the reputation it proudly wore. The recovery began shaping up rapidly, and Larry was running out of blockers by the time he crossed Oakman State's thirty-five-yard line. Finally he went down in a thundering tackle from the side.

Larry leaped to his feet quickly, tossed the ball to an official, and raised his clenched fists above his head. He was smiling as he ran to the huddle that was forming at midfield.

Chuck Pearce let out a long breath of air and relaxed. In the grandstands, all the fans stayed on their feet, sensing that what they had just seen was only the beginning and more was to come. High above the field in the press box, Bill Oliver also remained on his feet. He was smiling.

From one of the players at Pearce's left on the sideline, a loud voice rang out, "Hey, twinkle toes," and the entire Marlin State team sent up a laughing cheer.

As Larry leaned into the huddle to call the next play, Pearce spotted Jimmy Arnold on the far sideline. Arnold was barking into the ear of a heavyset lad who was nodding his head in sudden jerks. Clearly Jimmy Arnold realized that the jig was up, and he was sending in a linebacker to replace the extra defensive halfback who had been smothering the Tigers' passing attack.

"Did you know that was coming?" Cody asked, stepping alongside Pearce.

Pearce glanced at Cody, who was smiling. Pearce returned the smile. Yes, in a way, he thought, I did know it was coming. But he said, "No, Larry didn't tell me he was going to do it."

"Oakman State was as surprised as we were," Cody said.

"Yeah," Pearce answered.

On the field, the Oakman State linebacker was in the game now, gathering his teammates around him to relay the new defensive strategy from the coach. The extra defensive halfback was jogging to the bench.

As the Tigers broke out of the huddle to line up,

Pearce eyed the team closely. He thought he detected more spring in their step, more snap in their movements. They, too, had been surprised by Larry's call for a quarterback run, and it couldn't help but give them a psychological lift.

Larry's next play was essentially the same as the last one, only this time the running back circling wide for a pitchout was Burlington T. Johnson. Winnie was free to burst through the line and race to the sideline for a pass. Top priority went to the pass to Winnie. The quarterback ran only if he had to. And now, suddenly, the pass was a more formidable weapon than ever before, backed up by the threat of a quarterback run.

Larry took the snap from center, turned, and ran to his right. Johnson raced behind him, a little wider, with hand outstretched for the pitchout that never would come. Winnie slid through the line and turned on the speed, veering for the sideline.

Oakman State's zone defense shifted to cover Eddie Evans, floating out to the left, and sent a halfback peeling off to pick up Winnie, heading for the sideline.

Larry was outside his right end now. He flicked a fake pitchout to Johnson and looked for a second at Eddie Evans, and then turned his attention back downfield just as Winnie faked inside, cut back to the outside, and continued to tightrope down the sideline. Winnie's body fake gained him a half step on the lone defender, and Larry instantly rifled the ball downfield.

The pass was right on target, and Winnie gathered it in at the ten-yard line and scampered over the goal.

Larry never saw it. A tackler crashed into him the moment he let go of the ball, and he went down in a heap. But the roar from the Marlin State grandstand told the story, and Larry was smiling when he got up in time to see Winnie leaping, both hands stretched high in the air, in the end zone.

The lights on the scoreboard blinked 13-13.

Joe Talmadge hugged Larry. Chuck Pearce, who had stood up when the pass left Larry's hand, knelt back down on the sideline and chewed a blade of grass as Mitch Reynolds trotted onto the field for his kick.

The kick was good, 14-13.

chapter 22

By the time the Marlin State players got to their dressing room somebody had scrawled the final score in huge figures on the blackboard: 21-13.

Marlin State had added another touchdown in the waning minutes when a demoralized Oakman State team had been unable to stop the combination of Larry's pinpoint passes, his quick runs off tackle on the option play, and his pitchouts to Winnie and Johnson, mixed in with Louie Stetson's punishing plunges into the line.

Chuck Pearce was the last man into the dressing room. He closed the door behind him, leaving a throng of cheering fans, including an ecstatic Henry Osgood, outside in the corridor. For a moment Pearce watched his players—weary, dirty, but victorious. There's no picture like it, he thought, as he remembered his own days as a player and the exhilaration that overrides all fatigue when you've won the big one.

Harry Willis, who had never gotten off the bench through the entire game, was leading the celebration as usual, leaping around the dressing room slapping his teammates on the shoulder and whooping a war cry.

Pearce stepped onto a bench and raised his hands for silence. It took a moment for the players to calm down and turn to hear what he had to say. "You'll never forget this day, and neither will I," Pearce said.

The cheering erupted again.

Pearce stepped down off the bench and leaned over to catch the words of Jerry Phillips, the student manager, who was trying to make himself heard with a message above the din of the dressing room.

"There's a man named Brad Hudson outside," he said. "He told the guard on the door that you would want to know that he's here."

Pearce glanced around the dressing room, finally locating Larry, half out of his uniform in the midst of a group on the far side of the room. Larry was dirty and sweating, but he was smiling, and he was shouting something to Joe Talmadge, who was laughing.

"Okay," Pearce said to the student manager. "I'll handle it."

He walked to the door and opened it. When he gestured slightly, the cheering fans parted to make room for a man in the crowd.

Brad Hudson walked slowly, painfully, with the help of two aluminum crutches, moving through the crowd and through the door into the dressing room. Nobody in the crowd knew him. He was young, in his twenties, with a handsome face, and he wore a wide smile.

Pearce closed the door behind him.

Brad stopped and leaned heavily on the left crutch, letting go of the right crutch and extending his right hand to Pearce. "Hello, Coach."

"Hello, Brad. I'm glad you were here."

Some of the players noticed him. He was a stranger to them.

Then Larry blurted out, "Brad!"

The man on the crutches looked in the direction of the call and said, "Hi, Larry." He was smiling.

Larry stepped forward. "You were out there today?"

"Wouldn't have missed it for the world," he said.

Pearce turned to the players, now quietly lining the walls of lockers, and spoke slowly. "I want to introduce Brad Hudson," he said. "He's Larry's brother. Maybe you never heard of Brad Hudson, but he was headed for becoming an all-American at Southern Cal when he was injured. They told him he would never walk again. He has to use those crutches, but he fooled 'em, and he *is* walking again.

"It seems that beating the unbeatable is a Hudson family trait, both on the football field and off."

Larry looked from his brother to Pearce. "But how . . . ?"

Pearce smiled. "I told him you were playing, Larry. He had a right to know." Pearce paused and then added, "That was back when I didn't know myself whether you were really playing. But I had a feeling that you would come through today, and"—he looked at Brad—"I guess that Brad had the same feeling."

The room was silent.

Winnie stepped forward and shook Larry's hand

without speaking. Louie Stetson followed him. Pearce walked to the door, opened it, and let the shouting fans stream into the dressing room.

One man, a stranger, walked up to Pearce and said quietly, "My name is Roger Bledsoe. I represent the National Small College Bowl Association. I know it's still early in the season, but could we talk?"

"We can talk over here," Pearce said, and he led the man to a corner away from the celebrating fans and players.

About the Author

Thomas Dygard was born in Little Rock, Arkansas, and graduated from the University of Arkansas at Fayetteville. He began his career as a sports writer for the *Arkansas Gazette* in Little Rock and joined the Associated Press in 1954. Since then he has worked in Press offices in Detroit, Birmingham, New Orleans, and Indianapolis. At present, he is bureau chief in Chicago.

Mr. Dygard is married, has two children, and now lives in Arlington Heights, Illinois. He maintains his interest in many sports and occasionally plays tennis and handball.